JASMIN LACOSTE

C000052953

THE
FORGETFUL
RAIN

THE DARK DESERT SERIES
BOOK 1

To my mom, Ann. You always believed in me. I miss you every day.

And to my husband, Kyle. Thank you for being my biggest supporter. I love you.

CHAPTER 1

Rainy

We're running for our lives... And if they catch us, we're both dead.

***

My eyes open and are met with nothing but more darkness, making me question if I'd opened them at all. I try to move, but my body refuses, and violent pain bolts through me.

Using what little energy I have; I feel around the cold floor. It's damp and gritty, offering nothing more than a solid surface that leaves my fingers numb and my body shivering. I lie still, taking countless breaths to keep calm.

Slowly, I become familiar with the surrounding darkness. So much so that I question if it is all I've ever known or if this is death, and if so, would this be my eternity? Paralyzing pain and darkness? The thought petrifies me.

After a moment of despair, a rush of adrenaline surges through me. I refuse to accept this fate. *This can't be my reality.*

I urge myself to move, to defy the pain. I place my hands on the floor, forcing my body barely an inch off the ground, but the pain is unbearable and I instantly fall back down. I let out a small whimper as the stabbing pain intensifies, shooting through every one of my limbs and leaving me feeling weak and exhausted.

I lie still again, accepting defeat as I wait for the pain to pass. What could I have done to have ended up like this? Could this be Hell?

Hot tears pool around my eyes.

I have nothing. Not a single memory. Intense fear spreads through me. Anything is possible at this point.

How long have I been here? How long will I be left inside this darkness without answers?

Small whispers suddenly fill the space, distracting me from my dreadful thoughts. I stop breathing, partly in hope of making out the words to find answers but also in fear. The whispers continue unintelligibly back and forth between the space around me.

My body trembles as I try to work up the strength to speak.

"Hello?" I finally say. The sound of my own voice startles me with its unfamiliar pitch and sound.

The whispering stops abruptly, plaguing the room with silence again.

"Hello?" I repeat. It echoes off the walls.

"Shhh!" A voice whispers back with urgency, but it's too late.

A light flickers on, immediately blinding me. I squeeze my eyes shut. Somewhere, buttons are beeping, followed by a door creaking open. I force my eyes open, squinting through the blur as they slowly readjust to the light.

The room is smaller than I'd imagined, closed off by four concrete walls. Surrounding me are thick metal bars separating me from the rest of the room. Across is an identical cell holding a person I can't make out through blurred vision. I turn my head slightly, still unable to move my body, and see another cell separated from mine. It holds a cowering woman hiding her face behind long dark hair, huddled against the wall.

Across the room are six stairs that lead to an open door. A blurry orange figure steps through and makes its way down them. Once the figure is closer, I can make out their orange rubber suit, concealing their body and face, and the large gun strapped to their waist. They hold a clipboard and walk past each cell, writing something down while seeming to examine us one-by-one.

They stop in front of my cell and peer down at me. I can't make out their face through the rubber shield but black eyes stare into me, as black as the darkness that swallowed me whole only moments ago.

My skin grows colder as their eyes pierce through me, holding me captive with a stare that says, *you're mine and there's nothing you can do about it.* I try to look away but fear turns me into a statue, leaving me even more defenseless than before.

At last, they turn away, releasing me from their petrifying spell. They begin walking back toward the stairs where another orange figure stands in the entryway, gripping an even larger gun to their chest.

Panic begins to rise as I realize I'll soon be swallowed by the darkness again. The thought is crippling, even more so than the person's eyes, and even more so than any other possible outcome there might be. I swallow and yell out before they can reach the stairs.

"Wait!"

The orange suit pauses and turns to face me.

"Can you please tell me what's happening? Where are we?"

I hold my breath and brace myself for an answer. They say nothing and after a few moments, they step a few feet closer and point the barrel of their gun toward me.

"Do not speak!" The voice booms, echoing in my ears.

I freeze, and they turn back around to leave. My heart skitters through my chest but I can't give up now. I can't be left alone without answers again. I just can't.

"Please! I don't understand what's happening. Why can't I remember anything?" I beg.

The figure stops walking again but doesn't turn around. I wait for an answer but instead, a shooting pain bolts up from my lower back and courses through my entire body. The pain is unbearable, an electric current that causes all my limbs to spasm against the hard floor.

A scream rips through me. The room cuts in and out of my vision as my eyelids fight to stay open and I almost lose consciousness. *What is happening?*

Eventually, the shooting pain stops and leaves me paralyzed. Tears escape my eyes as they lock onto the orange figures, the side of my face stuck to the floor. I watch them leave.

The door slams behind them with a resounding thud, taking any light with it.

I close my eyes tightly, begging for any ounce of comfort or relief and wishing I could remember something, anything at all. I take small shallow breaths; each inhale a stabbing reminder. I wait, hoping I might hear the whispers again but they never come.

***

For a moment, I forget where I am. My eyes frantically scan the darkness as a single memory enters my mind. I try to take a deep breath to calm myself but the stabbing pain in my lower back returns. With it a quiet yelp escapes me.

With all my strength, I reach back to search for the source. I stretch until my fingers graze against something cold and solid. Everything is sensitive to the touch as I study it carefully with my fingertips. It feels like a long flexible tube is biting into the skin of my lower back. I attempt to grab and pull it free.

"Don't touch it!" A voice hisses quietly. I flinch and pull my hand away, blinking hard to urge my eyes to find anything other than darkness.

I wait for a few agonizing moments, my heartbeat thumping loud in my ears.

"What is it?" I whisper back, voice thick with desperation and louder than intended.

Seconds drag as I wait for an answer but it doesn't come.

"Please..." I can't take the silence anymore. I don't want to be left alone in this darkness knowing nothing.

"If you try to pull at it, it will shock you again," the whisper finally answers.

I cringe at the memory of my body flailing in pain on the hard floor. I turn my head toward the voice, assuming it came from the woman in the cell beside mine, but I can't be certain. The darkness makes it almost impossible to tell where anything is. It's so deafening that it nearly blinds the other senses, making me question what's left or right, up or down, how much time has passed and if it's day or night.

"Where are we?" I whisper back.

Shuffling fills the space to my right, like someone is scooting closer. "We don't know. Somewhere bad," the whisper responds, a breath away now.

My heart sinks into my stomach. I've known since I first woke that, wherever I was, it couldn't be good. But hearing it said out loud, and knowing it for certain, flushes me with an incomprehensible amount of dread.

I look toward the voice, tilting my head slightly until my eyes meet two glowing orbs, peering through the darkness and staring back at me.

I hold in a gasp as my eyes lock onto them, freezing me in place.

"Can— can you see me?" I ask.

The luminous eyes shift, dropping closer to mine.

"Yes... Don't worry. Your eyes will adjust— if you're lucky enough to be here that long," she says darkly.

I swallow small bits of air as I try to absorb her words. "Will my eyes glow like yours too?"

"Yes."

I lie still for a moment, unsure how to feel or respond. The thought of seeing past the darkness brings a small sense of comfort, but the feeling is short lived. I don't want to be here long enough to test her theory. I don't want to be in this place at all. Despite not having any memory, I know of the world outside of this dark room. I know what is real and not real. Glowing eyes and being able to see in the dark is not real. It's just not possible. But somehow it seems this dark place can bend reality.

I don't understand.

"How is that possible?"

I hear her body shift again, diverting her glowing eyes away from me and taking away my only source of light or direction. "Quiet now. They will be feeding us soon," she whispers quickly.

My stomach clenches at the thought of food, an empty throbbing pain. How long has it been since I've eaten? Why don't I know anything, even something as simple as that? Every moment that I spend in this place, my lack of knowledge becomes even more terrifying.

Silence fills the room, dragging time along with it. I close my eyes and count my breaths to keep track and distract my mind. It's all I have control over. I can't move, I can't talk, I can't do anything other than breathe and count. It's the only thing keeping me sane.

After breath number 2,403, the familiar beeping of buttons goes off in the distance and the lights flash on just as quickly. I lay frozen and watch as three orange figures come flooding in. Each carrying a tray as they make their way toward us.

CHAPTER 2

Maze

I stretch my arms up slowly toward the clear sky that seems to blanket over everything else in sight. If I lay on the ground long enough and avoid looking at anything else, eventually the sky engulfs me.

One moment, I'm watching my hands blend with the orange and blue hues of the setting sun, then the next nothing else exists and I am floating.

This has become a favorite pastime during these long yet fleeting summer days. In the evening, when the sun hangs low and is no longer blinding and the air decides to cool, I find myself drawn to this lovely escape where nothing else exists but me and the sky. It's as if I'm being whisked from the physical ground, pulled up and away from everything I've ever known. I wish this sensation would never end. But I can't stay out here forever.

I sigh and allow my arms to fall onto my chest. Just like that I am no longer floating.

Ignoring the slight ache in my back from lying on the hard ground too long, I struggle to sit up. The hazy world around me slowly comes back into view.

Here we go again... I dread the thought of going back inside. Once inside, reality will hit and it's a grueling cycle that never ends.

I've tried not to resent it, but it's hard not to let those feelings seep through sometimes. It's been over a year since I graduated high school. Back then, I believed I would be in college by this point, doing something with my life. But I don't have time for any of that. I can still hear the echoes of my mother's words— "Don't abandon us. You must step up for this family." This means working and ensuring the house doesn't burn down and my sister doesn't starve, while she disappears for days without a word.

I should have never expected anything more than this... this life. If you can even call it that.

I finally brace myself and reluctantly stand from my safe space by the side of the house, where moments ago I existed far away from this place.

Sluggishly, I walk to the sliding glass door and reach for it. I peel my gaze away and glance back to where I was just lying, envious of my body's imprint in the browned dead grass. With a sigh, I open the door and step inside.

Immediately, I'm welcomed by the cold gust from our old air conditioner perched in the window. Our home is small. Cigarette smoke and knock-off Febreze clings to the old furniture my mom has held onto for as long as I can remember. The walls are stained with a thin layer of yellow. I've lived here for most of my life and never complained, despite some of the comments I received from others in school. They mostly made fun of how I smelled, which made me drench myself in cheap perfume for years.

My feet drag to the kitchen. I search inside the cabinets and half-empty fridge while making a mental note to go grocery shopping soon.

"It looks like mac and cheese with hot dogs again." As soon as I mumble aloud to myself, Zaya comes running down the hall from her room. She apparently has supersonic hearing.

"I was wondering where you were!" She races toward me with the energy only a soon-to-be sixth grader can have.

She's never anything but upbeat and energetic, and sometimes I wish I had the energy to match hers. *She's the reason I stayed.*

I shrug. "Told you I can teleport."

With a giggle, she dismisses my poor attempt at messing with her. "What's for dinner?"

I glance at the box of mac and cheese in my hands. She likely already suspects what it is, but I humor her anyway. "I was thinking of making a rich elbow pasta with a delicate cheddar sauce, garnished with savory pork." I smirk, using my best fancy chef voice as I gesture to the box and hot dogs.

She laughs, mocking me. "I told you, Mazie. You don't sound like a chef!"

"And how would you know? Some say I'm the best chef in the world."

***

Zaya watches cartoons on the TV across the living room while waiting patiently at the table. Once I'm finished making dinner, I bring our bowls and sit across from her. She immediately starts shoveling spoonsful into her mouth, scarfing it down like it's her favorite meal— even though we have it for dinner at least twice a week. I love how she appreciates the small things.

Her dark brown hair sits messily in a ponytail over her shoulder. She's wearing an oversized t-shirt and sweats hanging loosely on her small frame. I watch as she struggles to keep her sleeves from falling off her shoulders. Most of her clothes were once mine and I have vague memories of wearing the same shirt two or three years ago. Of course, it fit me better then. It's a miracle if we get clothes that actually fit us. They're almost always either too big or too small, but no matter what, they are always hand-me-downs.

I make another mental note to remind her to take a shower tonight.

My eyes drift between her and the TV. It amazes me how much she looks like our mom. The long eyelashes, dark eyes, and rich brown complexion. Yet, she couldn't be more different from her. I, on the other hand, inherited more of my dad's features; dark curly hair, thick eyebrows over hazel eyes, and olive skin. At least, that's what my mom has told me all my life. I've never actually seen my dad or Zaya's. Neither of them decided to stick around. *Who could blame them?*

I take my last few bites and wash away the artificial cheese flavor with water. Zaya finishes hers as well, gets up, and grabs our bowls to take to the sink.

"Thank you so much for dinner, Mazie!" she yells while half skipping toward her room in a rush. She's been captivated by a new game on her phone for the last few weeks, and lately she likes to lock herself in her room and play for hours.

I feel like I rarely see her these days. We used to always hang out— binge-watch movies, and eat yummy but crappy food together. Or go on long walks to the gas station for Slurpee's and candy. But lately, she hasn't been interested in all that stuff... I guess she's growing up.

I hate it. Where does that leave me?

"Hey! Make sure to take a shower before you go to bed, okay?" I call back, trying to sound as nonchalant as possible to hide the hurt in my voice.

"Okay, *Mom*!" She grins before disappearing down the hall.

I shake my head, pushing away my slight annoyance and accepting the change for now. I have to sooner or later.

Scooting my chair back, I get up and head for the sink. I wash the dishes in silence and try to take the time to clear my mind, steering it away from the grueling tasks that await me tomorrow. I hear the shower turn on in the distance and am relieved, even though it's not often that she doesn't listen to me.

The steam rising up from the sink keeps me motivated to finish cleaning before the hot water runs out.

Bang!

The front door slams and I jump, splashing water onto myself. Too stunned to focus on the pain from the scalding liquid, I turn around to see my mom stumbling in. Without looking at me, she slumps onto the couch across the room.

I glare at the time on the oven —9:38pm— and roll my eyes. She usually isn't here until long after we're in bed— if she actually shows up at all.

I stomp over to her with a bowl of what is left of the mac and cheese and hot dogs and set it in front of her. She reeks of alcohol. Her eyelids are dark with messy makeup and aged by all her mistakes.

"What's this?" She looks down, slurring her words. Her accent sounds thicker than usual. *She's definitely drunk then...*

"Leftovers," I say, my voice flat.

She doesn't respond. She just collapses on her side and closes her eyes, leaving the food untouched. I walk back to the kitchen to grab a glass of water before bringing it over and setting it on the coffee table. The sound of her deep breathing tells me she is already asleep. I'm not surprised... We never talk anymore and it seems we rarely see each other now. I don't remember my mom and I ever being close, but the last couple of years she's been disappearing more and more, and sometimes I'm afraid she'll never come back.

I finish doing the dishes then turn off the lights. My eyes sweep over her body and of course, she's still asleep. I would think she looks almost innocent and kind-hearted if I didn't know any better. But despite her peaceful state, I know that isn't true. She can't fool me.

I sigh, grabbing a blanket from the side of the couch and gently laying it on top of her.

Why are you this way, Mom?

She doesn't move and once I'm reassured that she won't for a while, I make my way upstairs.

My room is the only one up here. It's what you would call a loft with three walls, no door, and one window. It used to be my mom's painting studio before Zaya was born, but mom doesn't paint anymore.

The room is plain with nothing particularly interesting or telling. The walls are bare except for a couple of Polaroid pictures of Zaya and me, and random writing here and there among the white texture. I've never been able to find "my style" or decide how to decorate it. I never really have the time either.

I change into blue shorts and a white tank top then shut off the lights. I collapse onto my mattress that sits in the middle of the room with no frame.

My eyes find my phone that has been forgotten, charging on the floor for most of the day. I pick it up.

Squinting at the bright screen, I scroll through my emails and social media, finding nothing of importance. I gave up trying to stay active on them a long time ago. I figured I could never keep up with the exciting lives of my peers. But sometimes I get curious and check on the people I used to be close to, making sure they're still doing well, or reminiscing on the memories we share.

Before I put my phone down, I set an alarm for 8:00am on full volume so that I'm not late for work. *I can't be late again.* They've already threatened to fire me twice. Sometimes it's just hard to wake up in the morning, well actually, most times. I've never been a morning person.

I set my phone down and hug the pillow beneath me. It's dark in my room. The only light is pouring in through the window from what I can only guess is light pollution emitting off the city. Luckily, we live far enough on the outskirts that I can still make out some of the stars. I watch them as my eyelids start to droop and I imagine myself existing elsewhere, as someone else. Someone who might look at these same stars and never find them as enchanting, because their own life might be far more flavorful. I wonder what a person's life like that might look like as I slowly drift off to sleep. *I will always love Nevada skies.*

CHAPTER 3

Rainy

An orange suit sets down a tray in front of me, but the rarity of vision distracts my gaze elsewhere. I scan the room with my eyes, taking in as much detail as possible.

My eyes adjust more quickly to the light than before. The cell containing me is completely bare other than jagged dark concrete and thick metal bars. There is not a single ounce of comfort in this place. I glance over to the woman in the cell next to mine.

She hunches over against the wall, much like before, but I can see her face more clearly now. Her straight black hair, thick with knots, blankets her body and lays in chaotic layers on the floor around her. Her eyes are slightly squinted with iris's as dark as crows. She glares wickedly at the orange suit in front of her.

She snatches a tray when it is set onto the ground. Bringing unknown food to her mouth and curling into herself as her eyes stay locked on the orange figures. She stares them down with an intense hatred.

The sound of hard plastic ricocheting off of a wall brings my attention forward. A tray is tossed out of the cell in front of me, sputtering onto the ground and landing at the orange suit's feet.

He comes into view more clearly, the person in the cell in front of mine. His eyes dance with mischief. I take in his face as a large malicious grin spreads across it. The look says that he has been waiting for this opportunity for a long time. An opportunity to disobey.

Something about him fills an odd feeling inside of me, strange and magnetic. I can't pinpoint what it is nor seem to get myself to look away.

"You can't make me eat this bullshit anymore!" He laughs out as he half-heartedly stands. "You just tell Cock-eye that he better give me something better to eat or else I'm outta this shithole again!" He grips the metal bars that contain him, sticking his face halfway between them.

He's mocking them without any fear. Tempting them without a care in the world. Part of me is envious of him. *How can he be so fearless in this place?* Though, I can't bear to see what's bound to come next.

For a moment, nothing happens. I hold my breath, hoping that they'll spare him with each passing second. I don't know who this man is or what gives him this strength, but a large part of me prays for his well-being, regardless. I pray that I won't have to watch him suffer through the same pain I had. But then I notice something as my eyes sweep over him.

Why doesn't he have a tube-*thing* connected to his back like the other woman and I?

In a swift motion, an orange figure steps closer to him, forcing a black stick inside his cell and thrusting it into his stomach. It makes a loud zapping sound as blue sparks fly and fall to the ground with each deafening jab.

He falls to his knees, laughing painfully as his arms wrap around his abdomen.

He looks up, his light brown eyes meeting mine as long locks of shaggy brown hair dance around his head to his shoulders. His brave smile quickly disappears as his eyes search mine for what feels like longer than a moment. I lie unmoving, completely captured by his stare.

Abruptly, he looks away, shifting his body away from me and leaning his back against the concrete wall.

I reluctantly follow suit, pulling my gaze away from him, and watch as the orange figures slowly retreat for the door. I panic, realizing I have completely forgotten about the tray set in front of me.

I reach for it, hoping to see the food before the lights disappear again. I beg my body to move, to inch forward. But just like that, I'm too late. Darkness swallows me as I hear the loud thud of the door closing, leaving me defeated as my body refuses to move off the cold hard floor, paralyzed by pain.

Tears sting my eyes, filling at the corners where gravity pulls them to the ground. The hunger-pains somersault inside my stomach as I try to urge myself to move.

Please... I can't go on like this.

I brace myself, placing my hands flat on the ground on either side of me. My arms shake as I gather every ounce of strength I have to push myself up. I get halfway there, excitement for success almost bouncing into my chest, when my elbows buckle and I collapse back to the ground.

Soft whimpers escape me as the weakness and hopelessness of it all overwhelms me. Nothing could be worse than this. The pain, the hunger, the darkness. Not knowing who or where I am. I couldn't imagine there being a place as horrifying as this.

"What's wrong?" A soft whisper fills the space in front of me, distracting me from my small cries.

"I'm so hungry... but I can't move." I sniffle back, feeling utterly pathetic.

"You can't reach the tray?"

"No," I answer.

He grows quiet for a moment. "Have you tried shimmying your body toward it?" There's a small hint of humor in his voice.

I let out a heavy sigh, not having the energy to entertain his idea or even attempt it. "No, I haven't. But I don't think that will work."

"So, you're just gonna give up then? That's stupid. You have to at least try. Do it," his whispers urge, leaving me no room to argue.

I breathe slowly, feeling the last of my tears trickle down my cheeks and onto the ground. The corners around my eyes beginning to dry.

I'm going to die here if I don't do something. The increasing pain in my stomach is making that horribly clear. Am I prepared to die? Am I prepared to give up?

His voice echoes through my mind with all the strength and defiance it held. *You can't give up.*

A sudden surge of energy pulses into me. An impossible amount of adrenaline and sudden belief in myself, fills every crevice of my body. *I can do this.* I suction the palms of my hands to the floor, giving myself leverage. I use the support to pull my body forward an inch. My heart begins racing.

This is actually working.

"There you go. See, you got it." His soft whisper drifts to me, increasing the new found energy coursing through me with every word.

I lift my head slightly and see his glowing eyes watching me through the darkness. I swallow hard, tinges of fear and fascination joining with the energy. My body shakes as I continue to use the strength from the palm of my hands to slowly slide myself forward.

After a few more agonizing pushes, my hand brushes against a solid object. My fingers analyze it for only a moment before I know for certain it is the tray. I carefully pull it toward me and stop myself from almost yelping with excitement.

I actually did it! I want to scream at the top of my lungs. This is the first good thing that has happened to me since I woke up in this place. It's so small, and yet I feel as though I've just ran an impossible race, and somehow succeeded. It gives me hope.

"There you go. I knew you could do it," he whispers.

His encouraging words almost bring tears to my eyes, but the hunger and weakness gnawing at my every limb distracts me from it. I feel around the tray's contents with my hand, hoping to find any indication of what they could be. One section of it is completely liquid. I lick my fingers and taste nothing. It's just water.

Water. Everything goes numb. It feels as though I can't bring my mouth to the tray to drink it fast enough. I almost didn't notice the tortured thirst, muted among all the hunger and pain. I bring the tray to my mouth and lift my chin to suck the water from it with my lips. It's unreal how the water feels filling my mouth and racing down my throat. Unfortunately, it's short lived. The water disappears after only a few gulps.

It's heartbreaking actually.

Once I lick the tray clean of every last bit of water, I feel for the rest of the contents. One part is slimy and the other feels chalky, like powder. I immediately stuff them both into my mouth, not giving myself a second more to care about what they could be.

The flavor of the odd substances is bland, almost bitter and fishy like seaweed. I swallow anyway, finishing every last bit.

My breathing turns ragged once I lick the entire tray clean three times over. I hadn't noticed how much energy I had used trying to move my entire body toward it before. My stomach growls and gurgles loudly, cramping with pain and begging me for more but there's nothing left.

I go limp against the floor, accepting the weakened hunger and the empty satisfaction. At least now I know that I am not completely helpless. I have proven that much to myself and am glad to learn something of value about the person I am. And I believe I have the boy across from me to thank for that.

"There now, you feel better?" he whispers to me as though he read my thoughts.

"Not really, but thank you," I whisper back.

"I know it's not exactly *fine dining*, but you can't be picky around here."

Says the guy who threw his tray and demanded to have something different...

"Just leave her alone, Ryder. Your jokes have caused enough trouble as it is." The woman's whisper cuts in.

Ryder... His name bounces around my head.

"It's okay," I whisper back. "It's better than silence." Anything is better than the silence.

"Ya see? She doesn't mind," Ryder snickers softly. "So, do you remember your name at all?"

I sniffle, hugging my arms around my head. "No. I can't remember anything."

"Typical," the woman blurts.

"Why?"

"They take away your memory when you're put in here. Only Ryder has been able to gain some of his memory back."

"Is that because he doesn't have a— *tube*-thing on his back?"

Ryder blurts out a quiet laugh. "No, those just don't work on me anymore. Same with the memory thing."

"Why's that?" I ask, eager for an answer.

"Because he's been here longer than any of us, I'm guessing," the woman answers for him.

"How long?"

"As long as I can remember," Ryder says in a voice that's much less cheery.

I inhale sharply. So many questions swarm my mind, bringing on a slight headache. "And you've gotten out before?" I ask, remembering what he had said earlier. I can hear him sigh, letting a few seconds drag on.

"Yeah, I have. But they caught me again eventually," he whispers somberly.

A sudden and urgent pressure screams inside my lower stomach, distracting me from all of my questions.

My eyes widen. "Um, where exactly do you guys go to the bathroom in here?"

They both make inaudible sounds. "I usually just go into the corner," the woman answers quickly.

"Same here," Ryder whispers after.

The room grows quiet.

God, I didn't think this could get any worse.

"And what, it just piles up on the floor?" I ask, trying to keep my voice down. I had wondered what that smell was... But I had more pressing matters to worry about before.

"They usually clean it up every time we're taken out of here," Ryder says.

"We get taken out? We get to leave from here?" I almost speak louder than a whisper as a burst of excitement shoots through me, distracting me completely from the horrors of the conversation we were having moments ago. The thought of seeing daylight or being able to walk or even run, being anywhere other than this dark room, feels like winning the lottery.

"Yeah, but it's nothing to be excited about," the woman mumbles, bursting my very fragile bubble.

"Why?"

"You'll learn soon enough. But worst of all, you'll meet Cock-eye."

CHAPTER 4

Maze

Ring! Ring! Ring!

I'm awakened by the loud obnoxious ringing coming from my phone. *But it's still dark.* In a half-asleep state, I quickly pick up the device to silence it, but it's not my alarm. It's an incoming call from Stacey.

Stacey was my best friend throughout most of school. We still talk sometimes, but not as often as we used to. Like most childhood friendships, ours has seemingly become nothing more than memories and the occasional "How are you?" text.

The last time I saw her was over a month ago when she caught me at work and tried to invite me to a party at her boyfriend's house. I couldn't go and she wasn't very happy about it, so I haven't heard from her since.

What did she expect me to do? Say fuck it and ditch work? Sometimes she really doesn't think things through...

My eyes sting as they try to adjust to the bright screen above me. 2:03am. Why would she be calling me at this time of night? My heart begins racing as I try to decipher all of the possibilities. *Is she hurt? Did something happen?* I quickly answer before my thoughts send me into a panic.

I clear my throat. "Hello?"

"Mazie! I'm so happy you answered. What are you doing right now?"

I shake my head in disbelief but I can't help but feel a tinge of happiness at hearing her voice. "Uh, sleeping."

"Listen, I know it's really late but summer is ending and I miss you. Like really, really miss you."

I grip the phone and can feel my heart tighten in unison. "I miss you too, Stacey."

"I know you've been really busy with work and everything else but I just couldn't live with myself if I didn't try to do something fun with you before I left for school again," she explains, and before I'm able to respond she continues.

"Listen, you can't say no to this. Okay?" She pauses for a moment. "I'm already outside waiting for you."

I gasp and get up to look out the window and there she is, leaning against her silver jeep parked out front, with the phone pressed to her ear.

I stare at her, my eyes bulging out of my head. *This can't be happening.* "I can't believe you."

She peers up at the window, a wide smile spreading across her face. "See you soon," and hangs up.

Stacey has always been this way for as long as I can remember. She's adventurous, spontaneous, and most of all, stubborn. Even so, I've always appreciated her constant encouragement throughout the years. Even when my anxiety and shyness were determined to hold me back and keep me from trying new things, she would always push me and wouldn't take no for an answer. She even managed to get me my first boyfriend in junior high despite the odds against me (I really wasn't the best-looking kid.) While she was the life of the party, I was her goofy sidekick who always stuck by her side.

Without her, school would have been lonely and miserable.

But things are different now... It hurts to admit that since then we have drifted apart. I blame myself mostly. She was always destined for bigger and greater things. After she left for college a year ago and I was stuck here, our relationship was never really the same.

I back away from the window, my stomach turning in knots, and my palms damp with sweat. It's been so long since I've done anything like this, something new or exciting. Am I really considering doing this? *Calling out of work is out of the question*, I remind myself.

"Shit," I whisper as I place my face into my already sweaty hands. If I don't go, I'm afraid that will be the end of mine and Stacey's friendship. There's only so much distance a friendship can take before it inevitably thins out into nothing.

Plus, she's not giving me much choice, as usual. I'm certain she won't leave until I go with her. That's just the sort of thing she'd do. *So stubborn.*

I take a deep breath and try to relax my heightened nerves. I want to do this. I have to, otherwise I don't know why, but I have a feeling I will regret it forever.

In a rush, I slide my phone into my shorts pocket before grabbing a thin jacket and my bag with my keys and other essentials. I tiptoe making my way down the stairs and am relieved when I see my mom's figure through the darkness still lying on the couch, asleep. I slip on my tennis shoes and peek inside Zaya's room to make sure she's also asleep.

Her door is already cracked, allowing me to peer inside and see her small frame bundled up comfortably on her bed. I'm glad she didn't witness the incident earlier. I've always tried desperately to shield her from the cruel reality that is our mother. She's smart though, eventually she'll catch on if she hasn't already. Our home-life isn't particularly the most *normal* situation, and I'm sure that will become more apparent to her the older she gets. The same way it did for me.

I make my way slowly to the front door and pause for a moment to allow my heart rate to settle. When I was younger, I thought that by the time I was eighteen I wouldn't have to sneak out anymore, and would be able to leave freely, that I could make my own decisions and come and go as I pleased.

Unfortunately, if that were the case, I probably would have never come back.

I take a deep breath and open the door, making sure it doesn't squeak on the way. I step out into the cool summer night and lock the door behind me.

Stacey looks beautiful as always. Her caramel hair curls into tight ringlets which levitate above her shoulders. Her big brown eyes match the color of her many dark freckles that sit in contrast to her light brown skin. She has the type of beauty even makeup can't duplicate. She's wearing a leather jacket and jeans, and suddenly I'm feeling underdressed for whatever we're about to take on.

She runs over and swoops me into her arms and soon my worries from before seem to slip away in her tall embrace.

"I'm so happy to see you!" she shouts.

"Shhh!" I hush with a wide grin. "I'm happy to see you too."

She lets go, dropping me back onto my feet, and walks over to the driver's side.

"This is gonna be so much fun. I can't wait to show you!"

I open the passenger door. "Where exactly are we going?"

"I heard about this really cool spot in the desert, and I was thinking we could have a big bonfire there and dance around it like the little goblins we are," she explains with a mischievous look. "Plus, we won't have to worry about cops, so I brought us some party juice." She motions toward the backseat and there sits a case of beer and energy drinks.

I look at the drinks and back at her as she wiggles her eyebrows. *Maybe this wasn't such a good idea...*

"Stacey, I can't stay out too late. I have work in the morning," I try to say sternly.

She purses her lips. "Then we can just stick to the energy drinks."

"Is this place far? Will we have time to get back here before the morning?" I ask, now a little more worried than before.

"Yes, don't worry. We will have more than enough time to get you back here before the *morning*," she says, exasperated. I'm not entirely convinced, but I don't argue.

She starts the car and soon we're on our way. I roll down the window and watch the houses illuminated by street lights with dead grass and the occasional palm tree quickly disappear into a vast dark desert. There's not a single car in sight, but that's not unusual. Most tourists and locals like to stay within the city limits and pretend they're not surrounded by nothingness.

I, on the other hand, have always felt drawn away from the city. I would get as far away from Las Vegas as possible if it were up to me.

Alternative rock plays softly on the radio as I realize that Stacey is being quieter than usual. Which is saying something because most of the time it's impossible to shut her up.

"So, how did you hear about this place?" I ask, trying to start up a conversation.

"A couple of Brandon's friends told me about it."

"Oh, how are you and Brandon doing?" I ask but soon after the words leave my mouth, her mood shifts and I immediately regret it.

"We broke up actually," she says matter-of-factly.

"Oh— I'm so sorry."

I had no idea. Best friends are supposed to know these things.

"It's okay. Shit happens." She shrugs it off and proceeds to turn up the volume on the radio. I look back toward the window and watch as the moon follows us and the large Joshua trees become more consistent.

Stacey and Brandon had been together for almost three years. I didn't know anyone else our age who had been together that long. Hell, I didn't know any adults who had been together as long. I can't help but think about all the girls in the movies and TV shows who are there for each other during break-ups, and how they watch chick-flicks and eat ice cream together. I feel like I've failed as a friend, once again.

Suddenly it occurs to me that maybe that is why Stacey wanted us to do this so badly. Perhaps this is her way of eating ice cream and watching chick-flicks? Relief washes over me at the thought. I'm happy that I did this. *I'm happy that I didn't let her down.*

The music blares as we drive deeper into the desert, the city lights far behind us now. Stacey's eyes stay glued to the road as she sings along to some of the songs while bobbing her head back and forth. I watch her with admiration. It's impossible to tell when something is really hurting her. She's probably one of the strongest people I've ever met, always turning a shitty situation into something fun or meaningful.

After a while, I lean my seat back and try to get comfortable. For now, I'll put all of my worries and responsibilities in the back of my mind and only focus on this moment. I never thought I would get to someday mend our friendship and turn it back into what it used to be— and right now it really does almost feel like old times.

A pleasant comfort lingers inside my stomach as I curl into the seat, hugging my legs and staring into the sky. There's always an odd familiar feeling that takes hold of me when I look up at it, but I tend not to question it because the answers don't exist. My eyelids grow heavier as I allow the vibrations from the car's movement to cradle my already exhausted mind. Then before I know it, I drift back to sleep.

CHAPTER 5

Rainy

"Cock-eye?" I repeat the words aloud, remembering that Ryder had said the same name during his outburst.

"He's the only other person you'll get to talk to here. He runs this place and he's the fucking worst," Ryder explains, bitterness and hatred coating his voice.

"What does he want with us?"

"I don't know. He does these weird tests and experiments on us but we've never figured out why." He pauses. "Just remember when you see him not to make him mad or provoke him. It'll just make it worse for ya."

The room grows quiet again following Ryder's dark warning. My heart pounds as I imagine what exactly these experiments might entail. I imagine some horrific dissection happening to my stomach or needles being put into my brain. The images make me dizzy but I try to stay calm. I need to distract myself.

"So uh, I know your name is Ryder, but what do I call you?" I direct the question to the woman in the cell beside me, using her glowing eyes as guidance.

She's quiet for a moment, long enough for me to think she won't respond, but then she answers. "Atlacoya, but you can call me Coya for short. It's the only name I know of because it's tattooed on my arm."

"That's lucky..." I trail off. I wish I had some indication of my name.

"Then how did you come up with the name 'Ryder'?" I glance back over to his glowing eyes across the room. Appreciation swims through me for the sense of direction in the darkness.

The room is quiet again but only for a moment.

"It's what they've always called me," he says.

"Who?"

"Cock-eye and everyone else here."

"Will they give me a name too?"

"No," Coya answers for him. "Ryder has been the only one."

"Oh... How long have you both been here?" I ask, almost afraid to hear the answer.

"For me, maybe years. For Ryder, maybe his whole life."

Ryder stays silent as Coya finishes speaking. I hold my breath; afraid the sound of my heart breaking can be heard within the concrete walls. The thought of being stuck here, like this, my whole life, is petrifying... Knowing they've both been here for who knows how long, with nothing but the sound of their own whispers. Forced to eat God-knows-what, and having to defecate on the floor only a few feet away from where they sleep. I cover my mouth to keep the sobs at bay. *This can't be happening. I can't do this.* The words repeat over and over in my head as my body begins to tremble with every silent sob.

"Trust me. It's never going to get better. It won't even get easier. You'll only get used to it, *if* you even get that far." Coya's cold words feel like sharp blades seeping into my chest. I hold my mouth closed tightly so as not to let out my cries. How can someone survive so long in this place?

After a while, I finally manage to calm myself. My tears form a puddle on the side of my face, bringing an even colder chill over my body. But I can finally breathe normally again, despite the remnants of clogged sniffles.

I dissect everything they've said so far, trying to piece it all together and figure out the truth of this place, and what this all means. "So, there were others then? What happened to them?"

"We don't know. They're here and then they're not. The others never stay as long as us," Coya explains, anger in her voice.

"They let them go?" My heart betrays me and quickens once more with hope. I should know better by now.

"No. Not likely... Be quiet now. They'll be back soon," she commands coldly.

"How do you know?"

"I just do. Now be quiet," she says quickly, without any more explanation. I exhale deeply, frustrated because I have so many more questions. I can't accept this as my life. *If others have been able to escape this place, I will too.*

I lay quietly, waiting for the hauntingly familiar sound of buttons beeping. When they finally come, the door opens but the lights never turn on. A tall dark figure takes a step through the threshold for no longer than a second before disappearing again. I take a breath of relief as soon as the door closes, feeling somewhat thankful for the darkness as opposed to the frightening possibilities *being taken* might bring.

***

It's been what feels like days since I've woken up in this place. I can't truly tell how much time has passed. My only sense of time is how much I fall asleep and wake up— which is often. Coya and Ryder haven't spoken more than a few words to me since I first arrived. I've tried to ask more questions but Coya just tells me to be quiet before we get caught again, leaving me alone in the darkness with my own thoughts.

I've screamed at the top of my lungs to combat the silence more than once, but that has only brought back the angry orange figures and the shooting pain from the tube at my back. The only way to escape the silence and darkness is in my sleep, or when the tall figure appears in the doorway occasionally, always just for a few seconds. *Watching over us...*

I could finally sit up when they brought us our second feeding, after —what I can only assume— days of agonizing hunger. I can't tell what's worse, the hunger, the pain, the absence of my memory, or the absolute hellscape that is this dark and silent room. All of it is agonizing.

At least now, I can do more than just lie in pain, waiting for the unknown and being completely helpless. Being able to sit up has been a small victory that I have felt grateful for for an immeasurable amount of time now.

I lick the damp gritty walls, savoring every drop of water that glides onto my tongue, tasting of earth and rock. It brings me the smallest bit of satisfaction.

God, I'm so thirsty. Once my tongue is raw and I'm certain I've covered every inch of what I can reach, I carefully lean my back against it— avoiding the portion where the tube meets skin— and rest my head.

I close my eyes for a moment and pretend I'm somewhere far away. I imagine my faint breathing is the sound of waves calmly crashing into sand. *In and out, in and out.* I feel somewhat at ease until the putrid smell of my own waste meets my nose, bringing me back to this hell and causing me to gag.

It takes everything in me to hold what little I have left in my stomach down. Even sitting on the farthest end of my cell doesn't protect me from the horrific odor.

I hunch over, covering my mouth and nose with my shirt. I let the drool drip from my lips as my mouth fills with saliva, and my stomach almost chucks what I imagine to be only dust and stomach acid by now. I sit like this for a while, arms inside my shirt, hugging my legs, keeping myself warm until the sound of the buttons beeping returns.

I jump as the door swings open and a group of orange figures storm in. They march tall with guns strapped to their chest, same as before, but this time, one stops at each of our cells and opens them. My eyes widen, fear freezing me in place as I realize it's finally happening. We're finally being taken. I can't bear to move or think about what might come next. All I've known in this place is darkness and fear, trying to imagine something more than that is almost impossible.

Swiftly and without warning, two orange figures step into my cell, grabbing me by my arms and pulling me to my feet. Their touch is rough and foreign, but I cannot focus on that for long. My knees immediately buckle, failing to hold me up. I fall back to the ground, all the muscles in my legs throbbing from the unknown excursion.

"Get up!" One of them commands

My body stays frozen to the ground, refusing to cooperate.

"I said get up!" The orange figure growls with an almost inhuman pitch. They grab me by my hair and pull me up with so much force I almost faint, before covering my head with a bag.

I don't have time to focus on the pain. Their sharp grip on my arms keeps me steady on my feet. I can't see anything but the ground as they drag me out of the room. I watch our feet move and the floor shift from the dark concrete to a shiny white colored tile before they finally sit me down and remove the bag.

Harsh bright light blinds me as I try to look around. Once the blurriness clears from my vision, I see that in front of me sits Ryder and to my right sits Coya. We're in a small narrow, brightly lit room with white walls that seem to emit the very light my eyes are sensitive to. We're sitting on long white benches protruding off the walls, and there doesn't seem to be a door. Not one that I can see anyway.

"What is this place?" I ask, trying to keep my voice steady as I take it all in.

"They put us in here sometimes before taking us into experiments." Ryder answers without opening his eyes. His head is leaned casually against the wall as though this is a relaxing moment for him.

"Why?"

"Probably to give us vitamin D or some shit. At the end of the day, they want us healthy enough for whatever they do to us," he explains calmly with a bit of impatience in his voice.

I glance at Coya. She rubs her arm and stares at the ground blankly. I can tell that neither one is interested in talking, so I give up. I lean back, allowing a small part of myself to at least enjoy the warmth of the walls and the clean air as I breathe in. So far this isn't nearly as horrible as I imagined. This room is actually quite nice once your eyes get used to the light. It's warm, bright, and clean...

After a while in silence, I break.

"What's the first thing you'd do if you got out of here?" I say aloud, hoping to spark their interest. I wait for their answer but after a few long moments, they give me none so I decide to answer myself instead.

"I'll tell you what I'd do. I'd get the biggest meal possible with every kind of food there is, and I'd eat until I couldn't eat anymore," I explain, my mouth watering with every word that slips out. I look up and see Ryder looking at me now, the corner of his mouth lifting slightly into a smirk.

Finally.

"I would look for my child," Coya's voice speaks up, taking me by surprise.

I turn to face her, stunned. "You have a child? How do you know?"

She wraps her hands protectively around her abdomen, and grips her stomach. Her eyes fill with an unbearable sadness. She then lifts her shirt to reveal her paled brown stomach, covered in thick beautiful stretch marks that streak across her skin, paired with one thick scar along the bottom.

"They're out there somewhere and someday I'll find them," she whispers softly, tugging her shirt back down. "These demons may have erased my child's face from my memory, but they could never erase my love for them."

My mouth goes dry and my throat constricts, choking, as I take in every one of her words. I try to speak but before I can say anything, the wall beside me shifts and opens.

CHAPTER 6

Maze

I jolt awake, sitting up quickly and forgetting where I am. My body is drenched in sweat and it's hard to breathe. I look around frantically, memory slowly coming back to me.

I'm in Stacey's car but Stacey is gone. I open the car door and peel myself off the sticky seat. I step out hoping to find some relief, but the blazing desert heat sucks the air right out of my lungs.

The sun immediately beats down on me with no remorse as I struggle to wipe the sweat off my body. My eyes search the area for Stacey but still she's nowhere in sight. There are no buildings, cars, or anything that would suggest humans have been here. Just a hauntingly barren land surrounding the cracked concrete road. I grab my phone from my pocket. 9:17am. *Shit. Shit. Shit.*

My face falls into my hands as I realize how truly fucked I am. I am most definitely fired. I can only hope there's some way to explain there was an emergency, or come up with some other excuse. My hands begin shaking as I realize what losing my job will do. No more food, no more electricity, at least not until I can find a new one.

I take a few deep breaths, the hot air burning my insides. *This is not okay. Where is Stacey?*

Not allowing myself to panic, I fumble with the phone in my hands, dial Stacey's number, and then press the phone to my ear.

"There's no service. I've already tried." Stacey's voice from behind me causes me to jump.

"Shit! You scared me! Where were you?"

She looks down at the phone in her hands. "I was trying to find a signal, but no luck." She shakes her head, obviously disappointed in herself.

"What even happened? Why are we out here and why the hell didn't you wake me up?" The questions spew from my lips.

"You're gonna think it's really stupid." She frowns.

"What happened?" I ask again, my voice sounding harsher than I intend.

She avoids looking at me. "After you fell asleep, I just kept driving and I wasn't really paying attention. Then before I knew it, I was lost and out of gas. I just thought I could find a signal and call a tow truck to pick us up before you woke up. I didn't wanna worry you. I'm so sorry Mazie." Her voice cracks into almost a sob.

At this point I don't know how to feel. I don't know if I should panic or comfort her. I know she didn't mean for this to happen, and that I shouldn't blame or lash out at her. It wouldn't help anyway, not in a situation like this. All we can really do now is try and get help. I let out a frustrated sigh and rub my increasingly sweaty forehead. "So, you don't have any idea where we are?" I ask, trying to sound as calm as possible.

She looks around as if our surroundings might reveal something they didn't before, and then back at me. "I'm pretty sure I saw a little town a couple of miles back that had a gas station," she says, sounding a little more confident now.

"Well good. At least now we know we're not completely in a scary movie scenario."

She gives me a slight smile before hugging me.

"Thank you for being you," she says before letting me go. We're both drenched in sweat and I'm suddenly very aware of how dry and parched my mouth is.

"Do you have some water? I feel like I'm dying."

She licks her lips at the thought, then walks over to her trunk. She opens it and rummages around for a bit. "I don't, but I do have half a bottle of Gatorade," she says apologetically. I pinch the bridge of my nose, trying to stay as patient as possible. *You would think that she would have thought to bring water, knowing she was practically kidnapping and dragging me out to the desert...*

She tosses me the bottle of red liquid. I open it and take a few gulps. It's sweet and very warm from sitting in a hot trunk for too long, but it offers some relief as it makes its way down my dry throat. I stop myself from drinking too much and hand it back to her, watching enviously as she drinks some as well. My thirst isn't satisfied but it will have to hold us over until we can reach the town.

We grab our bags from the car, making sure we have everything we need for this unpleasant trip we are about to embark on. Stacey grabs a couple of the energy drinks and beers, stuffing them into her large purse before swinging it over her shoulder. "You never know what might happen. Better to stay prepared." She shrugs jokingly. I roll my eyes. I don't have the energy to scold her.

The heat is almost unbearable, but luckily, we both have our sunglasses and can see easier despite the blinding sun.

We talk about everything to help distract us and pass the time. Stacey tells me about her college life and how it's nothing like how high school was. She says the classes are hard but being able to party at frats and sororities makes it all worth it. I'm not surprised when she tells me she chose to live in a dorm instead of a sorority. She never did do well with other girls trying to challenge her. She then goes on about the new friends she's made and how she wishes I was there too so I could meet them as well.

Abruptly, she stops walking.

"Brandon cheated on me."

I stare at her in disbelief at the statement and sudden change in conversation. I don't know why she waited until now to tell me. I never would have pegged Brandon to be that sort of guy. He always seemed to worship the very ground Stacey walked on.

"I'm so sorry, Stacey. Why didn't you tell me?"

Her lips quiver as she stares at the ground. "I didn't want to admit it, to myself or anyone... I just really thought we'd last, you know? But I guess the distance was too much for him." She pauses, then continues. "I thought I was good enough for him to wait. I just really thought he loved me." She shakes her head and wipes away a lone tear that manages to escape. I hug her again for as long as the heat will allow, then step back to look her in the eyes.

"You are good enough, okay? Fuck him and every other guy who can only think with their dicks. You're a goddess and he's the biggest dumb-ass who ever lived."

She lets out a sad laugh and nods her head. "Thank you, Maze," she says as we start walking again. I can't remember the last time I've seen Stacey cry or show any kind of true vulnerability. She's always been the one to put on a brave face and find the bright side to things. This entire experience she's shown me a completely different side to her. A side I hadn't known existed, but that I'm grateful to witness.

We continue walking for hours, occasionally stopping to rest and drink what's left of the Gatorade. Before I woke up, Stacey had changed into her 'workout outfit' of a matching gray sports bra and shorts that she luckily always keeps in her car. I'm just thankful I rolled out of bed in my blue shorts and tank-top and didn't change into anything else before I left.

We're doing everything possible to stay cool but I am feeling more than unsuccessful. It's a miracle that we both don't burn easily and grew up under the Las Vegas sun. Anyone else in our situation would probably look like a sun-dried tomato by now.

For once, I'm thankful to have grown up inside Satan's butthole.

Stacey collapses onto the dirt on the side of the road and pants with exhaustion. I don't want to point out that we haven't seen a single car this entire time and that I'm really starting to worry. Instead, I try my best to keep our spirits high.

"Looks like we have no other choice but to break into these bad boys," I say as I pull out the energy drinks from her purse. We each take one and begin chugging till they're empty. Stacey sighs as she wipes the drops of liquid from her mouth.

"We should have been there by now," she mutters.

I study her face, trying to come up with some words of encouragement but I'm coming up blank. I'm starting to lose my optimism as well. "You're sure you saw the town coming from this direction?" I ask.

She shakes her head in defeat. "I don't know anymore."

I scan our current surroundings and still there's no sign of people or houses, *no sign of hope.* Just miles and miles of desert and rocky mountain ridges in the distance.

I check my phone for what must be the millionth time and am only met with more disappointment. I stare at the words on the top left corner of the screen. "No service." My eyes linger for a while, staring at the wallpaper displaying a picture of me and Zaya. I took it a couple of months back when I allowed Zaya to do my makeup and it ended up being a messy disaster. She made me look like a clown. The picture was taken as we laughed hysterically at the sight of my face.

My heart hurts at the memory. *I need to get home.*

Stacey chews on her nails and looks lost in thought, staring off in the distance. "I think I recognize those mountains," she finally says, breaking the silence. She points toward the same far off rocky mountains I noticed before.

"You do?" I ask. *Has she lost her mind already?* From what I can tell, nothing sets them apart from all the other's we've passed.

She stares harder for a moment. "Yeah! I'm pretty sure those are the same mountains you drive past when going back to Vegas! Which would mean that the freeway is just on the other side of them and there will be tons of cars!" She stands up excitedly. "We could hitch a ride and get gas to bring back to the car!"

I rub my temples to ease a lingering headache now pounding from heat and dehydration. "So... You think we should walk over there?"

"I mean, I think it's our best option. We've been walking out here for hours now and haven't seen a single car or anything." She waves her arms in the air to everything surrounding us. "If we go that way, we could probably be at the freeway in an hour."

CHAPTER 7

Rainy

My body stiffens as the wall to my right separates and moves from its original place, creating a vacant pathway. A man steps through with an orange figure by his side.

The lanky man is dressed in a tight gray suit, neatly pressed to his body without a single wrinkle. His long arms are folded behind his back as he stands tall, bearing a wide smile that holds too many teeth. His skin is so pale it looks almost gray and waxy as it moves, resembling modeling clay. I stare at him in horror. One dark eye peers down on us as the other looks to the ground. *Cock-eye*.

His one working eye studies us slowly before he straightens his back out and clears his throat. "Let's take

51

the new one today," his nasally voice directs to the orange figure by his side.

Oh god no.

Within an instant, the orange suit grabs hold of my arm and pulls me to my wobbly feet and out to the other side of the wall. The wall shifts again, sealing us into a large, poorly lit room. I'm forced onto a chair that looks much like the chairs you'd lay on at a dentist office.

"Thank you. That'll be all," the man says, staring at me intently. The orange figure strides away and disappears through another hole in the wall.

The room has a strong stench of chemicals to it and is filled with tables scattered with unknown metal objects and machinery. Dim fluorescent lights hang from the ceiling, making the room feel uncomfortable.

I sit frozen, trying to keep calm. I keep my eyes away from the terrifying sickly pale man before he steps into view, forcing my attention on him. He swipes his slick dark hair back with one hand, despite it being flat to his head with a wet appearance.

"My name is Lionel Williams, but you may call me Doctor Williams." He introduces himself with an unnatural grin. His towering body moves along in an inhuman manner, looking sticklike as he speaks. "What would you like me to call you, hm?" He says with a patronizing tone.

I turn my head away, not wanting to entertain his question. This man is even more terrifying than I imagined he would be. After learning of him, I spent every waking moment fearing what he might be like and imagining what he might do to me once I was alone with him. Now that the moment has come, I can see I underestimated my own imagination.

But despite my fear, I can't seem to make my mouth move to answer him.

"Your time here will be much easier for you if you choose to cooperate." His voice grows darker as he crouches down low, forcing my gaze on him again. He shakes his head slowly; his lazy eye seemingly sways back and forth with each movement. Still, he grins wide and unnaturally, showing each and every one of his perfectly white and straight teeth.

"I don't know," I finally give in. "Call me whatever you want." My heart races as his one functioning eye stares at me. Every second that passes feels like a choice between life or death.

He straightens once more and strolls over to the other side of the room, rummaging through the different devices on a table in front of him. "Let's hope for your sake, you have enough satisfactory DNA," he mutters, loud enough for me to hear. My eyes widen as he turns back around to face me. He snaps rubber gloves over his hands and the sound is piercingly sharp, making me flinch. He then walks back over with a large needle in hand.

"What is that for?" I ask quickly, frightened beyond belief. My worst nightmare is coming true. *He's gonna stick needles in my brain.*

In one quick motion, he grabs hold of my arm and drives the needle into my flesh effortlessly without answering. I wince at the pain as he connects it to a clear tube attached to a large device on the table beside him. He sits down across from me, fidgeting with the buttons.

I watch dark blood pool into the clear tube and slowly make its way up into the odd device. My skin around the needle grows cold, making me lightheaded at the sight of it. I lean against the chair, failing to fight the weakness now taking over.

"Good now, just relax."

"Why are you doing this? Why am I here?" I ask, my voice sounding faint.

His eyes stay glued to the device, unmoving. "It would be better if you didn't ask questions." The words slither out of his mouth like venom. A clear warning.

The whites of his eyes grow large around his dark pupils before he stands abruptly. He grabs the device, bringing it close to his face as though he can't believe what he's seeing, almost yanking the needle out of my arm in the process. A low demonic laugh escapes his throat. He drops to his knees, bringing the device down with him and loosening its pull on the needle in my arm.

"This is magnificent! Absolutely magnificent!" he yells out, placing his hand on his face and letting out a humorless laugh.

I watch him carefully, unsure how to react to his sudden outburst. His drastic change in behavior makes him look like a completely different person compared to his dark controlled mannerisms from before, but it doesn't make him any less frightening.

He begins mumbling incoherently to himself as though he's inside his own world. I try to make out what he's saying but can only pick apart bits and pieces.

"This is more than any of the others... almost as much as him... the power... more than substantial..." He continues on, staring off into the distance. His cheeks have pulled into the inhuman grin and his one working eye is filled with crazed optimism. It makes my stomach twist with even more fear than before.

This can't be good...

I try to make sense of his words, putting the pieces together to try and understand their meaning, but it doesn't matter. Whatever he's discovered about my blood can only mean more pain for me, whether that be more experiments, or death. I don't want to be here long enough to find out. *I have to get out of here.*

My eyes frantically scan the room, searching for anything that might help me escape. Something tells me I won't get an opportunity like this again. He's not looking at me. There are no orange suits in sight, and for once my back is not connected to the electric tube. We might be alone in this room for now, but who knows for how much longer? I have to push through my fear; this could be my only chance.

I search the room quickly, sifting through the different scenarios.

I could use the clanky metal machine to my left and hit him in the head with it. It's only a few feet away... *No, it would be too heavy for me to carry. He would definitely overpower me and then, I'm dead...*

I could just try and make a run for it... *No. With those scarily long legs of his, he would definitely catch me and then once again, I'm dead...*

Or I could...

It then hits me.

I glance down at the thick needle inside my arm, causing every one of my nerves to heighten. I can still feel the blood leaving my vein, pushing through and up into the clear tube. It makes my head spin. I take small shallow breaths, trying almost unsuccessfully to mentally prepare myself for what I'm about to do. Oh god. *I have to do this.* I remind myself. *I may never get a chance like this again.*

Without giving myself another moment to back out, I brace myself and quickly rip the needle out of my arm. I stand to my feet and try to ignore the dizziness that blurs my vision and almost pushes me back down. Warm liquid trickles down my skin to my hand but I ignore it. Charging forward as quickly as I can, I jump toward Cock-eye, using all my strength and adrenaline. My arm lifts to stab him but it is a second too late. He turns facing me and blocks the blow with his arms. The needle pierces through his hand.

Shit. Shit. Shit.

I quickly turn away and run to the wall, feeling around the solid surface for a way out. My body shakes and trembles as I pat down every inch, unsure exactly what to look for to try and open the pathway to get out. *Shit, I didn't think this through enough!*

After a few unbearably long moments of searching, I pound my fists hard against the wall in defeat. What am I supposed to do now? Is this where I die? I can hear Cock-eye shuffling on the floor behind me. All the hairs on the back of my neck stand up. He really is going to kill me. *No.* This can't be the end. I have to at least try. I pound my fists against the walls again, punching and kicking with all my might. I use everything I have left in me until I can't anymore. My body gives up before I'm able to argue against it. I'm too weak... I fall to my knees, unable to hold myself up anymore despite how desperately I want to keep trying.

There's nothing. There's no way to find the opening. There's no way out of this.

Cock-eye lets out a low rumbling chuckle, and despite every nerve begging me not to, I slowly turn toward him. I'd rather stare death in the face when it inevitably takes me away. It's better than the blind anticipation, knowing it's about to come, but not knowing exactly when or how.

I watch as he gets back on his feet. He looks at his hand before pulling the needle out without even the smallest reaction. He watches intently as the blood drips down his palm and splatters onto the white tile floor. He then brings his hand to his mouth and slowly licks the blood away like it were a delectable chocolate to him.

His eye meets mine, hollow and lifeless yet dark and hateful. I can't seem to get myself to look away no matter how much I now want to. There's something sick and twisted about the way he watches me in this moment, as though he enjoys every bit of fear and confusion he inflicts upon me. He pulls his hand away, his eye never leaving mine. He stares me down with that same large and unnatural grin. The seconds tick by painfully as he savors the terrified look on my face.

"You are going to wish that you hadn't done that," he finally says in a low, taunting voice.

I watch in horror as the small stab wound on his hand sizzles and disappears, the blood flow ceasing as though it were never there.

What the hell!? How is that possible?

I can't get myself to move, even though alarm bells are ringing loudly in my ears, begging me to run or hide, to fight back, and do anything other than sit helplessly. But I just can't move.

This isn't right... *He isn't human.*

He puts his long arm back down to his side before slowly making his way toward me.

CHAPTER 8

Maze

I know she's probably right. The throbbing between my temples and the exhaustion plaguing my body is growing rapidly, making it hard to think. I'm not certain it's such a good idea for us to stray from the road, but if we don't get help soon, I don't know what will happen. Nothing good. The image of our withered dead bodies invades my mind. I try to push it away. *That can't happen to us, it just can't...*

I sigh. "Alright. Let's try to be quick."

Stacey jumps into action. "Onwards!"

She's much more lively now; the energy drink must have already kicked in. I can't say the same for myself as my body aches with each step I drag forward. We walk cautiously, watching the ground to avoid small cactuses and any snakes that might sneak up on us. That's the last thing we need is a lethal bite from a rattlesnake. I try to ignore the thought.

Walking feels a lot more challenging. I can't remember the last time I walked this much. I think it must have been back in sophomore year of high school. I had won an award for a painting I did and got to present it at an art gallery downtown.

I was so excited about it all week. My mom had assured me she would be there and we'd go home together when it was over. I took the city bus from school and stood proudly by my art as people flooded in and out to view mine and the many other pieces that other students were presenting.

I remember waiting patiently for hours. Never moving an inch in case my mom might miss me in the sea of people.

Once it got dark, the other students started packing up to leave but still I didn't move. I watched as everyone left, one by one, until I was the last one there. I didn't want to let go of the hope that she might still make it. But when the time hit 11pm, I was told the gallery was closed and that I had to go.

I slowly packed up my art and walked outside. I stood outside the gallery for a while, staring at all the parked cars in the parking lot for the slight possibility that she might be one of them, waiting for me. She wasn't, of course. I took the city bus as far as it would take me. But they stopped running at 12:30 and I was nowhere near my house. So, I walked the rest of the way home.

I guess I could have called someone and asked them to pick me up, but at the time I didn't know many people who had their driver's license, and I was too embarrassed. It took me probably three hours before I finally made it home. I was so exhausted and upset that I threw away my art piece. Out of resentment? I don't know. My mom never did tell me why she didn't make it. I never asked, and I never painted again.

Sometimes I think that was the tipping point of our relationship. That was the moment I realized that she really didn't care, and she was never going to change.

"We're almost there!" Stacey's excited voice brings me back to reality.

It's getting dark as we finally approach the rocky mountains. They're steep and bigger up close, towering over us against the setting sun.

I can't hear any cars...

"Well, let's get to the other side," Stacey says between pants. I can tell she's trying her best to remain in good spirits. I say nothing, holding my breath out of fear for what we'll find on the other side. *God, I just hope she's right.*

We walk slowly around the mountain-side, our bodies weak and exhausted. It feels like twenty minutes before we finally reach the other side of them.

Nothing but more desert stretching on for miles and miles. Shock and despair rise inside me as I stare ahead.

"Dammit! I can't believe this is happening!" Stacey yells out as she falls to her knees. I stare out, desperately searching for any sign of people or anything that could help us. What can we do? I try to think back to all the survival shows that Zaya and I would binge watch on the weekends, hoping to reveal anything that might be helpful to us. *What would Bear Grylls do?*

"We're gonna die out here," Stacey whispers, her body curling into itself.

"No, we're not! Don't say that! Don't even think like that." I snap, trying to ignore my pounding headache and the impending doom sitting in my stomach. "We're gonna figure this out, okay?" I try to convince her and myself. She curls deeper into her knees to hide her face and doesn't answer. I sit down beside her, rubbing her back while trying to come up with something.

It's dark now and the air is finally starting to cool, offering some relief. But there's no room for appreciation given our current situation.

Loud screams and yelps cut through the night from a distance. Startled, we cling to each other. We stay very still, petrified in the surrounding darkness. The screams sound haunting as they continue, getting louder by the second. "What is that, Maze?" Stacey whispers, trembling. Realization hits me.

"Definitely coyotes. That's the sound they make when they're killing something," I whisper without a second thought.

"That's not scary at all," she says sarcastically. Her body shakes but there's a small hint of relief in her voice.

I stand up quickly, ignoring all the nerves screaming not to. "We need to find a safe place to build a fire. It'll keep animals away and keep us warm tonight."

She hesitantly pulls herself up after me. I pull out my phone from my pocket and turn on the flashlight to help us navigate through the darkness. I hold her hand as we walk carefully, picking up small sticks and any flammable debris to build a fire with along the way.

After scouring the ground, we finally find a small clearing in the dirt. We hurriedly sit down across from each other. Stacey hands me the lighter from her bag, and I gather all our findings into a pile before putting the lighter to it. Thankfully it lights without a problem, and soon we have a decent fire and feel a little safer because of it.

We sit and stare at the flames in silence.

For a moment, I pretend that we are just camping like we have countless times in the past— before she left for college and before my life turned into a miserable routine. I pretend we're not stranded and that there isn't a possibility of death at the end of this... That this is just another innocent night of camping. For just a moment, I try to convince myself.

"What do you think everyone is thinking back home right now?" Stacey asks, interrupting my wishful daydream and bringing me back to reality.

I shrug. "I don't know. I didn't tell anyone where I was going." *And I could hit myself right now because of it.*

She sighs. "I didn't either. They'll probably think we ran away or something, once they figure out we're both gone."

No, not Zaya. Zaya would never think that. "I'm sure they're looking for us right now. They'll probably even send out a helicopter to search the desert." I try to think positively.

"I hope so... My parents are probably freaking out right now. They're already over protective as it is. I bet they won't even let me go back to school after this." She smirks. I'm happy she's gotten past the idea of us dying out here. I didn't want her to give up.

I fight back tears at the thought of what Zaya is going through right now. I don't want my mom filling her head with ideas and making her think I abandoned her. I know that's exactly what she'll do. I feel so angry and helpless not being there for her. Anything could happen without me there... *Please don't lose hope, Zaya.*

Stacey pulls out a beer from her bag and cracks it open.

"Hey! You can't drink that! It'll dehydrate you more."

She narrows her eyes at me. "It's all we have, Maze! And it's better than nothing." She starts chugging and disregards any objection I might have.

"It's only gonna make your pee taste worse when you eventually have to drink it..." I mutter.

She spits out the liquid from her mouth in a fit of coughs.

"Oh god. Please tell me we won't really have to do that." She stares at me with disgust.

I laugh. "Who knows. I've seen it done on survival shows."

"I would rather die."

We both grow quiet again. The frightening truth looms in the air between us; if we don't get help soon, we will die. It's getting harder to ignore that now.

I stare up at the night sky above us. It's bizarre how much more beautiful it is here, in a dark scary place, than in the safety of our city, muted by the lights of our homes; a double-edged sword.

I watch the stars, taking in their beauty and allowing them to distract me from the horrors of our situation. My eyes sweep over the sky, searching for solace like I have many times in the past. Suddenly my eyes fixate on a bright light shining in the distance behind Stacey. My heart flickers with hope.

"Stacey, do you see that light behind you?"

She turns around and gasps. "Yes! Oh my god, there are people over there!" We both quickly stand and begin running toward it. After a few steps, I realize that the light is further than it appears.

"Stacey, slow down! It's too dark."

She stops, allowing me to catch up to her. We both pull out our phones and turn on the flashlights. We begin walking fast toward it, when suddenly my phone dies.

"Dammit!"

"It's okay. We'll just use mine," Stacey says as she grabs my hand and leads the way.

We walk quickly toward the blurry light until we finally get close enough to make out what it is. The light is another fire but it's much larger than our own. Surrounding it are people, about five, and they're accompanied by a black SUV parked a bit further from them.

Our steps grow slower as we get closer to the scene. The five people are tall and appear to be men dressed in dark suits. Something about them seems off. *What are these men doing out here? What are they burning that requires such a large fire?*

Hope quickly turns to fear when the smell from the smoke reaches us. It's horrible, like burnt hair and something else, something rotten and wrong. I look more closely as the large fire engulfs a pile of lumps stacked on top of each other.

My stomach drops as I make out scattered arms, fingers, and legs, entwined together amongst the flames.

Oh god.

I can't seem to look away from the mound of burning limbs. My hand reaches aimlessly to grab Stacey's arm and stop her. She doesn't seem to notice what's happening. Before I can say anything, she yells. "Hey! Can you please help us?"

As soon as the words leave her mouth, the men turn toward us, revealing large guns strapped to their chests and their faces somehow completely expressionless and identical.

We need to run.

"Run!" I scream. I pull Stacey back in the direction we came and soon we're running for our lives. Stacey's hand releases from mine as we both struggle to run as fast as we can. I panic, trying desperately to keep up with her. My chest aches, making it hard to pull air into my lungs.

The sound of gunshots piercing the air makes my blood run cold, almost knocking me off my feet. I see Stacey fall to the ground ahead of me. A scream escapes me as I push myself forward, using what little strength I have left to reach her. *But I fail.* I lose my footing and everything goes black.

CHAPTER 9

Rainy

I squeeze my eyes shut, terrified to see what might come next. Is this the moment where I die? The brave face I tried so hard to plaster on has now disappeared. I can't face death like I had hoped, when death is as terrifying as this. This man is made up of nightmares, and I really wish that I wasn't stuck in this room with him.

A sharp pressure surges down my skull and makes its way through my entire body, increasing with each passing second.

I want to disappear. I want to be away from him and this horrible place.

Escape, Escape... ESCAPE.

I can hear Cock-eye creep closer. My skin prickles when I feel his hot breath brush against my skin. Any moment now he's going to do something unimaginable to me and there's nothing I can do to escape it. I'm completely alone and helpless. Same as always. The thought is as equally frustrating as it is frightening.

Escape, Escape...ESCAPE! The words scream inside my head. The pressure builds inside my skull almost unbearably and I can't stop it. The only other place I know of besides this room is the cold dark cell where I woke up and have been held since. I dread that place, but it's better than here, so I beg internally over and over that I could be back there, away from Cock-eye and this terrifying room.

I feel Cock-eye's long boney hands grab hold of my arms, but then release them not a second later. The pressure inside my skull stops abruptly, now feeling like an immense release.

Afraid to open my eyes, I suddenly can no longer hear or feel him near me. The air around me shifts from neutral and tepid to cold and humid.

For a moment I question whether or not I'm dead. My mind can't seem to process what just happened. I keep my eyes closed until quiet gasps fill the space near me. I slowly lift my eyelids and freeze with surprise. Cock-eye is nowhere to be seen and I'm once again surrounded by familiar darkness. Coya and Ryder's glowing eyes now stare at me, wide and full of shock.

"I... I don't understand," my whisper trails off. The fear and confusion, with a small hint of relief, brings tears to my eyes.

"The— The door!" Ryder whispers back with urgency.

It takes me a moment to process what he's talking about. My mind is so jumbled that I'm struggling to wrap it around everything that happened. I step forward and wave my arms in front of me. *Nothing.* The door to my cell is open.

"Hurry! Come open my door," Ryder yells, not bothering to keep his voice down.

"How? I can't see anything." I shake my head, frozen and discouraged by how my last attempt at escaping went.

"Just come closer!" he says, his words rushing out, his luminous eyes pleading with me.

I step closer, using the glow from his eyes for direction, holding my arms out in front of me to search for the bars to his cell. Once I feel the cold metal brush against my fingers and his glowing eyes are only a few inches away from my face, he grabs hold of my hands. I suck in my breath, surprised by the unfamiliar feeling of being touched harmlessly for the first time, and the unusual warmth of his skin. He gently guides my hands to the left and places them on what feels like a hard lever.

"Okay now, see if you can jimmy that thing open," he directs softly. I swallow hard, using all of my strength to pull and push. I wiggle the lever up and down, trying every maneuver possible. Panic rises inside me when it doesn't budge in the slightest.

"It won't work. She needs a key to unlock it," Coya whispers harshly.

"It doesn't hurt to try," Ryder hisses back.

"Yes, it does! Because if she gets caught–"

Her words are cut off as the light flickers on, blinding the three of us. The door flies open and Cock-eye comes storming in. His lengthy body is frigid with anger. I back away from Ryder's cell, my feet almost failing as I trip over them.

"You!" Cock-eye charges toward me, hatred spewing from his lips and his eyes bulging out of his head. I stumble backwards into my cell before falling to the ground. He reaches me and stands over my fallen body. I lay speechless and wide-eyed as he bares his teeth with a crazed look on his face. He looks like a completely different person to the one I met in the experiment room not too long ago. He was calmer and more composed then. Even after I stabbed him, his unnatural smile left his face. But now, there is true anger in his eyes and it seems he can barely contain it.

Whatever I did to end up back here has really pissed him off.

"You worthless... Low-level lifeform... Disgusting creature. You think you can defy me?" He spits, his voice growing louder with each insult. He stands over me, waiting for an answer, but the room sits in paralyzed silence. After a moment, I think he will say more, but instead he leans down, grabbing my hair to hold me in place. I try to jerk away from him, not realizing what he's about to do. Suddenly I feel the sharp familiar pain in my lower back as he jabs the tube back in. I shriek in intense pain that blurs my vision and causes my body to tense, before I go limp against the floor.

"Good luck trying to warp now," he whispers to himself. It's so quiet I almost don't hear it through my ragged breathing as I try to get through the pain. Finally, he steps away from me, closing my cell door behind him.

I watch him pace the room back and forth while chewing his thumbnail. His eye shoots between the three of us, watching us madly as though he's thinking of what to do with us next. He stops abruptly and stares at the ground. I brace myself in case he might do something else horrible, but instead he rushes out the door, leaving us alone in the dark.

***

The room is eerily quiet after he leaves. This is how I imagine it sounds after an earthquake, tsunami, or any other natural disaster. *Deathly silent.* I stop myself from whimpering despite the pain. *I'm tired of feeling weak.* I force myself up into a sitting position, ignoring every throbbing ache coursing through me.

"I'm sorry... I'm sorry I couldn't get it open," I whisper between labored breaths. Shame and fear sting my eyes as I realize I blew probably the best opportunity we had at escaping.

"Don't worry about that now. What's important is how the hell you just... appeared in here!" Ryder whispers back with astonishment.

I shake my head. I wish I had an answer but I don't. Everything happened so fast. I thought for sure that I would die, but instead I ended up here again, and I have no idea how or why. I don't understand anything about this place or myself. Here the impossible is somehow possible and that only makes it more frustrating. Maybe in another scenario some would find it fascinating. Unfortunately, it only makes this place that much more confusing and terrifying.

Glowing eyes, stab wounds miraculously healing, and what I think is teleporting? What's next, flying?

"I don't know," I finally say. "I was just scared and wanted to escape, then suddenly I was here," I try to explain the best I can, recounting what happened.

"That's it? You were just scared?"

"Yeah, I mean, Cock-eye was going to hurt me because I stabbed him in the hand trying to escape," I whisper, almost embarrassed as I remember how it played out. I was stupid for trying.

"You did what!?" Coya's voice chimes in with disbelief.

"Badass..." Ryder chuckles softly to himself before he pauses and thinks for a moment. "So, if you wanted to escape so bad, why didn't you just transport yourself out of this place?"

I bite my cheek, disappointed that that hadn't been the case. "I don't know. I wanted to disappear to somewhere else so bad, anywhere but there. But the only other place I know of is *here*."

"Hmm..."

"The real question is, *why* wasn't Cock-eye surprised that this happened? He was more angry than anything. And why didn't he just kill you after everything you've done?" Coya questions coldly, in almost an accusation.

I hold my breath as her words start to fill me with a sense of guilt.

"Ignore her," Ryder interrupts. "She's just upset because everyone else brought here who did something wrong was killed on the spot. Except me, and now you."

My eyes widen at that, fear bouncing into my stomach. What does that mean? Everyone else has been killed, except me... and him? My mind begins racing as I try to desperately understand what this all means.

"She is right though. He definitely didn't seem *surprised* by what happened. Which is... weird." His words bring me back to the present.

I try to shake my mind of all the thoughts of death and instead my mind reels back to what Cock-eye whispered to himself before he left. "He said something about me being unable to *warp* again when he was putting the tube back on me."

"Hm, so he knows what it is then," Ryder whispers.

"*Warp, warp, warp.*" He plays with the word in his mouth. "You think you could figure out how to do it again?"

The thought brings me the smallest bit of hope quickly replaced by fear, as I remember how my last two attempts at escaping went. Each has failed miserably and has left me in an even worse position than before. The throbbing ache in my lower back is a painful reminder of that.

Plus, the thought of being killed if I'm caught again is terrifying...*but could it really be worse than this?* Who's to say if Cock-eye isn't already plotting all of the horrible ways he plans to kill me. If it's true what Ryder said, then I will probably be dead soon.

Exhausted by my fear and failures, I lay down on my side. I curl into my favorite position— the only position that keeps me warm in this cold desolate place. "I don't know," I finally say, not wanting to entertain the possibility any longer. Ryder sighs and turns his glowing eyes away from me, as if he can tell I'm not up to speak about it anymore.

The room grows silent again and with every breath I count, my eyelids grow heavier. Soon the darkness in the room morphs into the darkness within my mind, drowning out my thoughts.

***

I look around and can see nothing but darkness and twinkling lights in the distance. My body seemingly floats within its space, bringing me a sense of comfort I have never felt. I don't question it, and instead I allow myself to drift.

"Welcome back," a voice that seems to carry many voices, speaks inside my head and all around me. At first, I'm startled by it, but the fear quickly dissipates.

"Back?" I repeat. "Where am I?"

All at once, the voices respond. "You are nowhere, and everywhere. Where everything begins and ends. Where everything exists and doesn't."

CHAPTER 10

Maze

Darkness... So much darkness and pain.

***

Where am I? I don't exactly remember waking up. I don't exactly remember anything. I sit up and cough for some time, gasping for air. Beads of sweat drip down my face and onto the ground. It's so dry. It's so hot and my body aches all over.

I look around and there's nothing. Just dirt, and more dirt, and some plants and rocks, and— *oh look a rabbit!*

The gray rabbit freezes as it watches me attempt to stand before it hops away. Sharp pains and weakness spread throughout my body, causing me to sway as I slowly struggle to my feet. It takes everything in me to try and keep balance.

The rabbit seems to disappear among the brush. I don't follow it. Instead, I decide it's better to try to find food and water. Anything to make these uncomfortable feelings and pains go away.

I glance down and study my hands and clothes. My hands look bizarre and unfamiliar. My body and clothes are caked with dirt and muck, making the uncomfortable feelings double. I try not to dwell on it too long.

I need food and water...

I begin walking with no real destination. The aches inside my body throb in protest but I push myself forward anyway.

After a painfully long time, I finally come upon a long straight road that seems to lay out to the ends of the earth. I walk it for what feels like forever, hoping I might find where it ends.

My feet drag along the dusty asphalt. Ahead of me are mirages of water, glistening against the sun rays. I walk toward them, bursts of hope and constant thirst leading the way. But no matter how far I walk, or how close I get to them, the farther the waving mirages float away. Betraying me. Every. Single. Time.

I know they're not real, I know this. And yet, I have nothing else. Nothing to keep me going. Nothing to distract me from these pains. And so, I keep moving forward.

Curiously, I hear a soft humming coming from behind me. I turn around and sure enough, there's a blurry object making its way toward my direction. I stand and wait until the large truck comes into view, its engine growing louder the closer it gets.

I stand unmoving until it comes to a complete stop right in front of me. A round man hops out and stares at me suspiciously.

"What the hell are you standing in the middle of the road for?"

I contemplate his question for a few moments.

"I'm trying to find food and water," I finally say, the sound of my voice taking me by surprise.

He stares at me and seems impatient. "Well, you're not gonna find any out here. It's out of the way but I can take you to the cafe a few miles out."

He has a funny accent. I don't move. I just continue standing in place.

"Listen girl, you're gonna get yourself killed out here so you might as well just trust me."

I don't want to be killed...

I nod and walk over to the passenger side of his truck. The inside feels nice and cool against my skin and I'm happy to finally be out of the miserable heat.

"You want some water?" The man reaches back, grabs a plastic bottle, and hands it to me. "Here."

I open it and chug the entire thing within a matter of seconds. The water coats my dry throat and I'm finally starting to feel some relief as it makes its way down.

I look at the man when I finish and he eyes me suspiciously again. "What were you doing out here anyway?"

My heart sinks low into my stomach as I try to think of an answer.

Why can't I remember anything?

I glance out the window and trace my finger along the glass, searching for a memory. "I don't know."

He huffs. "Yeah well, I guess it's none of my business anyway." He pulls a cigarette out from behind his ear and lights it. I scrunch my face at the smell.

"You smoke?" he asks.

I shake my head.

He shrugs. "Suit yourself."

We arrive at a little old shack of a cafe in the middle of nowhere. A couple of cars are in front, and another large truck is on the side. "Well, here you are." The man nods me out. I open the door and hop outside, flinching as the heat smacks into my skin.

"Oh, and miss—" I look up at him as he eyes me up and down, his face twisted into a scowl. "Lay off the drugs."

Confused, I shut the door and watch as the truck pulls off and drives away.

A man slumps against the front of the cafe, gray hair caked with muck, and his clothes muted into shades of browns and greens from years of dust. He looks as dirty as I am.

Am I like this man?

He doesn't move as I walk past him.

The cafe looks a bit nicer on the inside, swarming me with the enticing smell of bacon and coffee. Eight red tables are lining the walls with windows beside them to look out.

I walk up to the counter and wait until the only waitress approaches me. She's an older woman with bleached blonde hair and dark makeup. She gives me a strange look. "What can I get ya, honey?"

I look up at the menu above her head and try to read through it quickly. *What do I even like?* My mouth waters at the thought of every option as I read. "Uh, could I get some pancakes and waffles with bacon, eggs and hash browns? Oh, and sausage!" The words leave my mouth before I'm able to stop myself.

She laughs. "Wow, someone's hungry." She writes it all down on her little notepad in front of her. "Alright, that'll be 36.50."

My breathing stops as I check my pockets. I have nothing. *Crap, I didn't think this through.* "Uh, I don't have any money."

She crosses her arms, annoyed. "Well then we can't help ya here. You can go find yourself somewhere else to freeload." She turns to walk away. My stomach clenches with hunger as I start to panic.

"It's alright, I got the bill," a young man's voice drags my attention behind me as he rests his hand on my shoulder. He's tall with sun-kissed skin, shaggy brownish hair and light brown eyes. He's wearing dusty jean shorts and an olive-green t-shirt. His face is round with a single dimple on one cheek that deepens as he smiles down at me.

The lady snorts and takes his money. "Alright, have a seat. It'll be out in a few."

Why did he do that?

I sit down at the far end table and to my surprise he follows behind and sits across from me. "Thanks, I guess."

He smiles again, a warm, genuine smile.

"Don't mention it. You looked hungry." He runs his hand through his hair and taps the table a few times as if he's thinking of what to say next. "My name's Ryder. What's yours?"

I look around the small restaurant and try to think back as hard as I can, with no luck.

"I don't know honestly," I finally say, feeling defeated.

He furrows his brows. "You don't know? What, did you forget it?"

I shrug. "I have no idea." He gives me that same strange look as the man from the truck, making me feel slightly uncomfortable. *I can't be that much of a freakshow, can I?*

"Then what am I supposed to call ya?"

I shrug again. *What is this guy's deal?*

"Hm," he thinks for a moment. "Well until you can *remember*, I'll just call ya Rainy, cause I miss the rain."

He thinks I'm lying. "Fine by me," I say, not caring what he calls me. Soon the lady brings the food over and sets it down. It covers almost the entire table.

"Jeez, you sure did order a lot." He gapes at all the food in front of us. I'm overwhelmed with hunger as I ignore his comment and spoon as much as I can into my mouth. Everything tastes so delicious. I take bite after bite, unable to slow down.

"You're not even gonna put syrup on those?" He eyes the dry pancakes I've already eaten half of. I swallow what's in my mouth, grab the syrup from the end of the table, and pour it on what remains of the pancakes. He watches me as I eat, and takes a couple pieces of bacon for himself.

"So, what are you doing after this?" he asks as he takes a bite of the bacon in his hand.

"I don't know. I haven't thought that far ahead," I say with my mouth full.

He smirks again and shakes his head.

"You're full of mystery, Rainy. I like it." He finishes off the bacon. "Would you maybe wanna join me for a swim at the reservoir?"

I swallow the food in my mouth and am finally starting to feel satisfied, my stomach feeling like it could burst. I haven't even eaten half of the food in front of us. The thought of it going to waste makes me feel like crying.

"There's a reservoir out here?" I ask as I try to force down another bite.

He half-heartedly gasps. "What? You never heard of Pahranagat Lake?"

I shake my head. *I don't even know my own name...*

"It's the best lake for swimming, even though you aren't *technically* allowed to swim there." He winks. "Plus, there's showers and bathrooms there, which... I'm guessing you might need."

I follow his gaze and glance down at my dirty hands and clothes. He's right. It looks like I've never had a shower in my life.

I think hard for a moment, weighing out my options. *Follow this strange guy to the lake or walk aimlessly through the desert again?* I suppress a shudder at the thought of the second option.

He seems harmless enough, and he did just buy me food.

"Alright, I'll go with you."

He slaps a hand on the table enthusiastically. "Sweet! And don't worry. I'm not a serial killer or anything." He winks again. I roll my eyes. I'm not entirely sure I should trust him but his presence feels genuine —as genuine as a weirdo in the middle of nowhere can be, I guess— and it seems I have no other choice at this point.

I box all the left-overs before we stand from the table and walk outside. He leads me to an old van on the side of the cafe. It's a reddish color, browned from rust with a white top.

"And this is my baby." He caresses the side of it. "She's from the sixties but she's never let me down. We've been through a lot of adventures together." He smiles at it fondly.

He opens up the passenger door for me and I lift myself inside. It has an older smell but seems comfortable and cozy, with a cream-colored rug interior. I look around and in the back there's a bed and wooden cubbies next to it with a pile of clothes and other miscellaneous things. He hops into the driver seat beside me.

"Do you live inside here?" I ask, motioning to the back.

He starts the engine.

"Yup! I'm what you would call a *traveler,* so this is my humble abode."

***

I can see him looking at me in the corner of my eye as he's driving. I can't figure out his deal and why he's being so nice to me. *Maybe he's lonely.* I imagine it can get lonely being by yourself, traveling from place to place. I wonder if I was a traveler too and got lost and forgot everything. *I wonder if I was lonely too.*

The Forgetful Rain

We drive for some time while he plays old-school music on the radio. He tells me about his many adventures, driving through all the states.

"What state are we in now?" I ask.

He shoots me a concerned look. "We're in Nevada."

I look around, taking in the vast desert as if seeing it for the very first time. It's hard to appreciate its beauty when you wake up in it with no idea how you got there, and feeling on the verge of starvation or heat stroke.

"It's really pretty. I like how the sky goes on forever."

His concerned look quickly disappears into a wide grin.

"Well, you'd love my favorite lookout. At night you can see everything."

CHAPTER 11

Rainy

My body floats effortlessly within the comforting darkness. Though, it doesn't feel like my body at all, and this isn't the same chilling darkness that encloses me inside the four concrete walls and metal bars. It's a familiar darkness that fills me with a feeling of security, a feeling of *home.*

"I don't understand." My voice calls back. The twinkling lights in the distance flutter with every word I speak. Despite not knowing where I am or what's happening, this place has an odd peacefulness to it. It makes me feel complete and a part of it. Part of me hopes that I am somehow dead and that this is my new reality. The comfort and peace here is not something I can ever remember feeling before, and I'm certain I would never feel back in that *place*. The sudden memory of it causes me to shutter. *I don't ever want to go back there.*

"It seems you have finally released the ancient part of your Being, to finally return here." The voices answer with a warm intensity that embraces me and sends goosebumps throughout my skin— or what feels like my skin. "It's been a long time since you graced this realm. Though, it appears your memory has been damaged."

"Yes, I can't remember anything." I speak quickly, trying to understand the meaning behind what the voices are saying. "Am I dead?"

A rumbling symphony of laughter fills the space all around me, causing the twinkling lights to sparkle in a chaotic sequence and the air to vibrate joyously. The deep darkness between the vibrant balls of light grows smaller with every burst of laughter. After a long few moments, it finally dies down.

"What is death if not merely a phase onto the next? A peaceful slumber followed by birth? No, death is not real. You are in the In Between. It is here where all thoughts materialize and energy is harvested."

It's hard to decipher the voice's words while still basking in the mystical comfort they bring me. I can feel myself getting pulled into the gentle warmth of the darkness. It feels as though my entire body is submerged under warm water, drifting within the current without the fear of drowning.

Everything about this place feels just right, and every single part of myself never wants to leave... Almost every part. Sadly, my trance is rudely interrupted by the memories of the dark cell, Cock-eye, and all of the mystery behind who I am. I have to know the truth behind all of the suffering. There has to be a reason for it all.

"Why am I here? Who are you?" The questions escape my mouth. The sound of my voice seems to ring through the air. Not exactly an echo. It moves in almost physically visible waves, as though it has a life of its own.

"I can be anyone or anything you want me to be. I can be a horse..." A large gray horse materializes before me as the voices speak, making me yelp with surprise.

"Or a tree..." The voices continue as the horse transforms and a towering magnificent Pine tree takes its place. It instantly takes my breath away with its size.

"A human woman... or perhaps a man." The many voices morph into one as the tree then takes the form of a naked woman and then a man.

My mouth gapes open as I watch the different forms appear like magic. I have never seen anything like it. All I've ever known is that dark horrific place. Until now, I never knew a place like this existed. A place so peaceful and familiar, yet magical and mysterious.

I really don't want to leave. My soul feels so deeply attached to this place.

I try to divert my eyes from the naked man who has appeared in front of me. My mind can't seem to comprehend what the man looks like, or how he is standing perfectly straight in the dark atmosphere, though it lacks solid ground.

"No, that's alright," I try to say but my voice comes out as a squeak.

As if he were commanded, the naked man disappears into nothing, leaving me once again alone in the twinkling darkness.

"As for why you are here, you are an Interdimensional being, not bound by any single physical reality or notion. It seems you have awakened that which has been dormant and allows you to come here." The voices continue on, answering my earlier question and radiating with a vibrational power as they speak.

"Interdimensional being?" I repeat back.

"Yes. Your kind has dwindled and is slowly dying out. Those who remain have been dispersing to different planets and realities, forgetting who they are and blending to survive. It's been such a very, very long time since one of you has come here. Your soul has beckoned you."

A painful wave of emotion washes over me as the voices finish speaking. I'm not sure why hearing this makes me feel so upset.

"But why? Why do we need to forget and hide... Why are we dying out?" My voice chokes as I try to fight the lump in my throat. The truth of the voices' words rings loud in my ears.

"There are other beings in existence who are incapable of the same empathy or abilities as you. Because of this, they have tried to use your kind for power. They have found ways to manipulate other planets and control them specifically to find you and others like you. However, your kind has been blending in with the species of other planets for thousands of years. Very few of you left have as much ancient blood as yourself."

Fear jumps into my stomach with an unnatural force at the realization. Everything that has happened since I woke up in that horrible place begins to play out in my mind in slow motion. It all makes sense now... Ryder, Coya, and I being held captive. All of the "experiments." Cock-eye and all of the orange suits. *They are the other Beings.*

I can't stay here. I need to get back. All of the others who have already been killed... If we don't find a way out soon, that will soon be us too.

Intense emotional pain envelopes me within the darkness, making it no longer feel like the peaceful comforting place it once was. I try to calm myself down, but a visible string of energy suddenly surges through me and sucks into my body from the dark atmosphere, as though it were being pulled into me like a vacuum with a magnetic force. Unable to stop it or control my emotions, my body pulsates with an indescribable power, causing the twinkling lights surrounding me to dim.

The power is almost unbearable for me to take. It fills my body more and more with each painful, angry emotion that swims through me in response to the dreadful truth.

"Calm yourself, *Undine*," The Voices command. "That is enough!" The energy coursing through me instantly escapes my body, being sucked back into the atmosphere from where it came.

I gasp, inhaling deep gulps of calming air and feeling sudden relief.

The peaceful warmth returns over my body and cradles me with a loving embrace that brings tears to my eyes. It soothes every negative emotion I felt moments before. I allow myself to sob within it, releasing the heavy burden within myself and feeling safe and loved in the process. If I'm being honest with myself, if it weren't for the others' lives being at stake, I would never leave.

After a long moment, I reluctantly gather back my strength as I realize exactly what I must do. My body may be nonexistent in this place, yet it feels like it is now standing on high alert. Confidence is racing through me with a new found certainty of the truth for who I am. *Who we are.* Ryder and Coya's faces flood my mind. All of their hopes and dreams, everything they endured before I came, and after.

I have to get us out of there.

"Those other Beings you spoke of, I think they have me and others like me. How do we escape them?" I ask with urgency.

"Remember who you are. You are capable of many things." The voices answer but they sound further away now. I can feel myself start to fade which brings panic to me.

"Wait please!" I yell out. I try to think of what to say next. There's so much more that I still don't know and that I want to ask, but I'm fading more rapidly with each passing second.

"Could you please tell me my name?" I ask before I completely disappear. I'm not sure why I ask it, but it feels important— like I'm taking back a small part of myself that I've lost and forgotten.

"Let's see...The last time you appeared here, it was Rainy, of the Nixie."

***

My eyes fly open as I sit up quickly. The familiar smell of wet rock and waste meets my nose, but the room is somehow different. Coya and Ryder stare back at me, but their eyes are no longer glowing. I glance around the now gray toned room, looking at the small details I could never see before. The glistening concrete walls, slick from the humid air. The long tube connected to mine and Coya's back, that sticks into the ground. The shorts and tank top I'm wearing, and never got a good look at.

My eyes fall on Ryder as he crawls closer to the bars of his cell and stares into me with his mouth hanging open. I hadn't gotten a chance to get a very good look at him either, and while I can't see color past the gray hues, I can see that his brown eyes are light and kind. His long hair frames his face in messy waves and his features are soft, but handsome. *He's beautiful.* I can't help but think that maybe the connection I feel between him and I is all because of who we are...*We're the same.*

"*No way.*" He mouths the words. "I'm guessing by the way you're looking at me that you can see me? Your eyes have already adjusted?" Ryder whispers softly, his voice lacking its usual sarcasm and humor.

"That's impossible." Coya's voice snaps. "No one's eyes have ever adjusted that quickly."

"Yeah well, no one else has ever teleported either. Or *warp*, whatever the hell it's called," Ryder argues, his sarcastic tone returning.

I look between them; a new feeling of closeness consumes me as I let the words from the voices repeat in my head. Knowing the truth has made me feel closer to them. We're here because we're the same. Not only that, but it also makes me want to protect them. It's not just about escaping by myself anymore. I need to get us all out of here.

They are my *kind* after all.

"Listen, I need to tell you both something really important," I begin. They both snap their heads in my direction, staring at me intently. Being able to finally see them and know that they're listening, it's a bizarre breath of fresh air— if that were to exist in this place.

I take a moment, thinking of how to word it. "I learned the truth... of who we are and what they are doing to us here."

I explain everything that happened at the 'In Between' and everything the voices had told me. They stare at me dumbfounded as I finish, their eyes somehow even wider than when I had *warped*.

The room is silent for a moment as they take in everything I've said. I almost fear that they won't believe me.

"How do we know it's true?" Coya finally says.

Ryder rubs the back of his head, his brows pinched together. "Don't be stupid, Coya. After everything that's happened, how could it not be true," he whispers sternly. Coya glares at him but says nothing in protest.

"I want to get us all out of here. Now that we know the truth, we might actually have a chance!" I whisper excitedly to hopefully lift their spirits.

"Just because you have these *special* powers, doesn't mean we do," Coya whispers coldly, dismissing me.

"Weren't you listening? We all—" I begin but Ryder quickly interrupts.

"I do," he says suddenly. We both stare at him.

"What do you mean, *you* do?" Coya asks slowly. Ryder sighs, hiding his face from us as he stares at the ground. His voice drifts to us slowly.

"When I had escaped, I met a man who let me stay with him for a while. I learned that he was really sick and so I started taking care of him. The doctors said that he was gonna die but— But when I went to him on his deathbed to say goodbye, something happened... He healed somehow after I touched him." Ryder finishes, staring off in the distance.

After a few moments of more silence, I finally speak. "You see, we're all the same. We can all get out of here," I whisper softly, looking back to Coya.

The Forgetful Rain

She shakes her head in defeat before finally giving in. "Okay, *Rainy*. What's the plan then?"

CHAPTER 12

Maze

We arrive at a lake that looks like an oasis surrounded by an otherwise lifeless land. Luscious trees grow along the water and random designated camp spots are scattered against the edge. Ryder parks the van in one of the campsites and we hop out.

"Wow. I would have never guessed something like this exists out here." I look around, stunned by the greenery that is so out of place.

"Yeah, it's a wildlife reserve so the government takes real good care of it."

Ryder leads me to what seems to be our own private beach along the water, tucked away below the campsite.

"This is beautiful." I stare out at the large body of water glistening in the sun. Large desert hills in the distance hover over everything, making it feel as though we appeared in a completely different world.

Ducks swim in circles while birds fly overhead, swooping into the water before returning to the sky. How a place like this could exist out here, flourishing with so much life, I don't understand. I guess that just goes to show how much difference water can truly make.

I watch Ryder as he takes his shirt off, tossing it to the ground before he runs into the lake without any hesitation. He dives in effortlessly and disappears for a moment before popping back to the surface.

"Come on! You gonna get in or what?" he shouts with a teasing tone.

I eagerly take my dirty tennis shoes off before slowly dipping my feet then easing my way in. The water is a gentle lukewarm temperature, and soft squishy mud molds between my toes, sending excited shivers down my spine.

I sigh, allowing my body to float and ease tension from the soreness and aches still lingering inside my muscles. "You were right. I really did need this."

He splashes water at me playfully. "I told you! That's why you should always trust me."

I can't help but giggle as he dives back into the water. I wait for him to pop back up to the surface, but he doesn't until he suddenly reemerges right in front of me with a mischievous grin plastered on his face.

"What?"

"Bet you can't beat me at water tag."

I eye him carefully, unsure of what he's getting at. But before I can get a word out, he picks me up and throws me into the water.

I jump back up, stunned and gasping for air. Again, he's out of sight. Then just as quickly as I realize what game he's trying to play; he pops back up in front of me once again.

A playful scream escapes my lungs as I try to swim away, but he catches me easily and throws me into the water again.

Something about Ryder makes me feel comfortable and safe. We play like carefree children until the sun starts to set, and it almost makes me forget that I don't remember who I am.

***

I'm sitting on the shore, soaking wet while Ryder carries wood over from the van to build a fire.

A nice breeze has picked up, sending chills and goosebumps along my wet skin as the sun disappears behind the hills.

Ryder sets the wood down and tosses to me a bundle of clothing. "I figured you might need these since you don't have any other clothes with you."

I look down and inspect the red t-shirt and flannel boxers in my hands. "Oh, thank you." I'm not sure what else to say.

He smiles a warm smile that I'm quickly becoming familiar with. "Don't mention it. It's not often that I get to play such a worthy Marco Polo opponent."

I grin at the memory of us playing just moments before.

"There's a bathroom down the road with a shower. I can show ya if you like?"

Eagerly, I nod, and he leads me to a small building. I step inside. The bathroom is small with one shower, a toilet, and sink. I undress from my wet clothes and put them into the sink before turning on the shower. I wait for the water to get warm and steam to fill up the small bathroom then I slip inside the stream.

The hot water feels heavenly as it runs down my body. I close my eyes and allow it to run over my face, completely relaxing my nerves for the first time since I woke up today.

I look down and observe myself as the dirt washes away. *This is my body.* It's a bit too thin and pale despite waking up underneath the sun.

My skin is sensitive to the touch as my fingers glide to my face and slowly trace down my neck and onto my chest. I cup my breasts and then trace my fingers down my stomach to my legs. Everything feels so foreign, yet familiar at the same time. I study every inch, getting to know my own body as if it weren't my own and belonged to somebody else.

I could stay like this forever.

I take my time washing the dirt away before reluctantly turning off the water and stepping out.

As the drops drip away from my body, I sneak a glance at myself in the mirror above the sink and quickly look away. This has been my biggest fear. I've been avoiding looking at my face all day, afraid that when I see it, I won't recognize it. Afraid that I truly won't remember a single thing of who I am.

I inhale deeply and walk over to the sink, staring at the soaked clothes inside. I turn it on and wring them out, washing the dirt and muck off the white tank top and blue shorts— the articles of clothing that are the only evidence of the person I was before today.

I have to remember.

I turn off the faucet and slowly peek up at the mirror in front of me. I stare at myself and a stranger stares back. I don't recognize the dark curls, the brownish-green eyes, the pink lips, nothing. You could have shown me a picture of this face before now and I would not have known it was me. I place a hand on my cheek and watch the reflection follow as if I can catch it making a mistake. *Who is this person? Who am I?*

My throat swells as I step back from the mirror and lean against the wall. What does this mean? What am I supposed to do if I can't remember who I am? Like the tears in my eyes, I fall to the floor.

Do I go to the police? What would I say? What is someone supposed to do in this situation?

A soft tapping sound comes from the door. I don't look up, afraid to face my reality.

"Rainy? It's been a while. Are you okay in there?" Ryder's voice calls from behind the door. Still, I don't answer and pull my legs to my chest.

I can hear the door open a crack before his loud footsteps rush in. He places a gentle hand on my shoulder. "Hey what happened? Are you okay?"

I shake my head, burying my face deeper into my knees. "I don't recognize my face... I don't remember anything. I thought I would at least recognize my face." I sob, afraid to look up and see that same strange look everyone has given me all day.

He rubs the small of my back softly and a sharp pain shoots through me. I wince.

"I'm so sorry." He looks behind me and gasps. "Jesus, what happened to your back?"

I finally look up at him. "I don't know. I didn't know it was hurt until you touched it."

He grabs the shirt he gave me from off the floor and hands it to me so I can cover myself. I then realize I'm still naked and we're in this small bathroom with the door shut. I ignore the thought and take the shirt from him, covering the front of my body as I stand and turn to look at my back in the mirror.

My eyes widen at the sight of it. A large bruise wraps around the bottom portion of my back. It's a dark purple color, almost black and spreads over every inch.

"I had no idea this was here..." My voice says below a whisper.

Ryder stares at it through the mirror then locks eyes with me. "You really don't remember anything... Do you?"

I turn to face him. "That's what I've been trying to tell you. I woke up in the middle of the desert today and can't remember a single thing. Every time I try to think back, my mind comes up completely blank." I try to keep my voice down as emotion threatens to take over again.

He rubs his head and thinks for a moment. "Do you think someone might have done this to you? That someone might have hurt you and left you in the desert?"

I clutch the shirt tighter to my chest. "I don't know... It's possible."

He looks worried now. "Do you remember where you woke up? Did you have anything with you?"

I shake my head. "No, I woke up and walked for a long time until I was picked up by a trucker who took me to the cafe. All I had were the clothes I was wearing."

He closes his eyes as if the thought is painful.

"I'm sorry I didn't believe you. I honestly just thought you were trying to play hard to get." He lets out a sad laugh. "It makes more sense now though. I thought it was weird that a girl as pretty as you was alone at that cafe with no money and covered in dirt."

His words make me smile slightly despite the situation. "Yeah well, seems everyone else did too."

Ryder walks toward the door. "Sorry, I'll let you get dressed." He shuts the door behind him, leaving me alone with my thoughts again.

I get dressed slowly and try to avoid thinking about all the possibilities of what could have happened to me. Freaking myself out more is not gonna help right now.

I leave the bathroom and walk back toward the campsite carrying my wet clothes. It's dark now. Ryder sits next to the fire, poking it with a stick until he realizes I'm back and stands up.

"Oh good, they fit!"

I look down at the clothes he gave me. The shirt is long and goes to my knees like a dress and the boxers are a bit loose but aren't falling down.

"Yeah, thank you again," I say, my cheeks turning hot as I sit down across from him and welcome the warmth from the fire.

"I'm sorry I didn't have a towel for you. I usually let the heat dry me off during the day," he says apologetically, obviously trying to keep the conversation light.

I shrug. "It's okay, I'm just happy I got to shower." My own stench was bugging me.

He smiles slightly and stares at me passed the flames. "Are you hungry?" He pulls out two plastic-wrapped sandwiches from a cooler beside him that I hadn't noticed before. "They're from the gas station, so they're not the best, but they're better than nothing. I actually kinda like them, but that's me. Pick your poison, ham or turkey?" He holds them out and I eye them.

"Hm... I don't know."

His eyes widen. "You mean to tell me you don't even remember what kind of sandwich you like?"

I sigh. "I mean, I know what they are but I can't remember what I prefer." This whole memory thing makes no sense to me. I know what everything is, what things are called, what they taste, smell, sound, look like, but I have no specific memories of them.

Ryder laughs and shakes his head. "Man, that's sure gonna make it tough on me when I take you on a date." He winks. "I'll tell you what, you can take a bite of both and decide which one you like best, okay?"

My cheeks flush but I try to ignore his comment. *Again, what is this guy's deal?*

He hands me the sandwiches. I open them both and take a bite of each. They're both delicious but I decide on turkey. The soft bread and cheese pairs well with the processed meat and are a welcomed distraction from what happened earlier in the bathroom.

"So, I was thinking," Ryder begins with his mouth full as he chews on his thoughts. "I really think it's possible that someone might have hurt you and left you in the desert. I also think it's possible that it was most likely someone in your life that you were trying to get away from." His voice grows serious as he tries to explain.

I swallow the food in my mouth, no longer hungry and frozen by his words. "Maybe you didn't have a good living situation and things got bad," he adds. "It's the only scenario that makes sense to me."

I don't want to admit that the same thought has also been in the back of my mind. Before seeing the bruise, I hadn't given myself much time to dwell on the possibilities of what could have happened to me. But after discovering it, I'm certain that the truth is something I'd rather not know. That the truth is something I was better off forgetting...

"Yeah, I've been thinking the same thing." I manage to say, barely able to keep my voice steady.

Ryder nods and takes a deep breath. "So, I've also been thinking. I would like for you to stay with me. You definitely don't have to if you don't want to! I just thought— I haven't had such great company in such a long time..." he says quickly, as though he's been working up the courage for a while.

I look at him in disbelief, surprised that he would offer something so big to a complete stranger.

"Are you sure? You really don't have to—"

He interrupts before I can finish. "Listen, I want to. I would rather you stay with me than have to figure everything out on your own. What kind of person would I be if I left you to fend for yourself in this mysterious world?" He smiles kindly.

The familiar feeling of my throat swelling returns and I want to burst into tears of relief that I met someone as kind as Ryder, and that I won't have to be alone to try to build a new life by myself. Or maybe worse, regain my old one.

"I'm really happy I met you," I whisper, swallowing the lump in my throat.

"I'm happy I met you too, Rainy." His voice is warm and sincere. Orange flames dance in the reflection of his eyes and I have to force myself not to get lost in them.

I think about the name he's given me, and how it's the only name I now know for myself. *Rainy*. I wonder what my name might have been before today. Would it have been as fitting and oddly familiar?

"Man, the stars look amazing tonight." Ryder interrupts my thoughts and I follow his gaze, looking up at the sky. I'm quickly filled with a sensation of peace as I scan through the countless balls of light. They scatter endlessly, leaving almost not a single space of darkness.

We stare at the stars for a while and I'm almost lost in a trance as a euphoric feeling hangs over me, whisking me away from the physical. Ryder sighs deeply, bringing me back down to earth.

"This is my favorite part of being a traveler, the freedom to enjoy the simple pleasures this planet has to offer." He closes his eyes with appreciation. I take advantage of the moment to study his relaxed face and admittedly handsome features.

He opens his eyes again and I have to peel my gaze away and return it to the flames. "What else do you like about being a traveler?" I ask, trying to distract myself. He answers without a beat.

"Everything. There's nothing better. I get to live by my own rules, my own schedule, and explore what's real."

"What's real?"

He nods, his eyes now gleaming brightly with passion.

"Yeah, what's real! Everyone in society is expected to live and do the same exact thing. Work to live and live to work, and we're shamed if we disagree with it. I couldn't stand it." He shakes his head. "I didn't wanna work till I'm old and gray and regret everything. That's not a real life to live." He waves his arms up, gesturing to everything around us. "This is what's real, living life free with no obligations."

I watch him and can feel his words vibrate within me. Then I think back to what I had thought about before when we were in the van. "Do you ever get lonely though?"

He quickly looks up at me, paused by my question.

"Traveling alone, I mean."

He contemplates for a moment. "I wasn't always alone," he begins, grabbing the stick and poking the fire again. "I used to have a dog named Dude. He was my best friend and was with me everywhere I went."

"What happened to him?"

"He died a couple of months ago of old age." He smiles sadly. "He lived a good long life and I'm just happy he spent it with me. He would have liked you, I'm sure of it."

"I wish I could have met him," I say to reassure him.

"I'll show you a picture of him the next time I turn on my phone." He smiles more joyfully now.

A phone?

"You have a phone?"

He shrugs. "Yeah, it's hard to live without one these days, but I only really use it in case of an emergency and to save pictures."

That makes sense. Ryder seems to definitely be a 'live in the moment' type of guy. It's odd not knowing if I had a phone or what happened to it.

Suddenly, a large lizard scurries from the bushes and onto my leg. I'm not startled by it; instead, an odd sense of joy comes over me.

"That's amazing! I see bearded dragons out here all the time but I've never seen one get so close," Ryder whispers, his voice filled with awe..

I slowly lift my hand and caress softly down its back with one finger causing it to return into the bushes just as quickly as it came. "Wow, Rainy. You didn't tell me you were a Disney princess!" Ryder says the name he's given me as naturally as he breathes, his eyes wide with amusement.

I shake my head and laugh, feeling lighter and more carefree. Maybe this won't be as bad as I expect it to be. And maybe he isn't as weird as I thought he was. It just felt hard to trust someone as kind as he is.

He stretches his arms and yawns.

"Man, what an insane day."

I sigh. "It's definitely been a long one that's for sure." *Especially since it's the only one I can remember.*

A sudden awkwardness takes over me as I realize we'll have to go to bed soon and I have no idea what our sleeping arrangements might be. I'm not sure how comfortable I would feel sleeping next to him. There's only so much room in that van. The vulnerability turns my cheeks hot.

"Don't worry, I'll sleep out here tonight and you can sleep in the van," he says as if he can read my mind.

I let out a breath of relief that quickly turns to guilt. "Are you sure? You're already doing so much for me. I'd hate to kick you out of your own bed."

He shakes his head. "Don't worry about it. I like sleeping outside anyway. Gives me more time to watch the stars," he assures me. "Plus, I want you to be comfortable."

I watch him walk back to the van and grab a sleeping bag for himself, and for whatever reason beyond me, I'm almost disappointed that we'll be sleeping separately.

He lays the sleeping bag down a few feet from the fire and walks me back to the van. "Tomorrow, I'll take you to my favorite lookout." He grins, letting me inside. "Just holler if you need anything, okay? Sleep tight, gorgeous," he says quickly, filling my stomach with butterflies.

"Okay, you too. Uh, g'night." I stumble over my words before he shuts the door.

I lay down gently, ignoring the stabbing pain in my lower back. The bed feels like a fluffy cloud as I settle myself in, allowing my body to relax. The blanket and pillows smell of sweet patchouli and musk and I'm soon feeling regretful that I didn't let him sleep beside me, where he could be near and I could feel his warmth.

God, I barely know him...

I barely know myself.

I try to clear my mind of it and the many events that took place today as I urge myself to fall asleep.

CHAPTER 13

Rainy

I lean my head against the damp concrete wall, closing my eyes to try and pick apart my brain for anything that might help us escape. Searching for the answers within myself just as the voices said to.

In the back of my mind, I worry that my whole experience at the In Between was just a dream and that all of this is for nothing. I worry that maybe there is no way of escaping and we're completely alone. But then I remember the peace I felt there, and there's no way I could have made all that up. *It just has to be true...*

I search my mind until my head starts to hurt before finally opening my eyes to give it a rest.

The three of us have gone back and forth discussing what we know and don't know, searching for any clue that might help our chances. What we know is that the tubes on mine and Coya's backs somehow prevent us from *warping,* and that we are in some way valuable to Cock-eye and the rest of our captors— which means that they most likely won't hurt us, at least not enough to kill us. *We hope.* We also know that we might have abilities that could help us escape and have agreed that we should do our best to keep it hidden from the orange suits, and prevent them from finding out that we know the truth.

This time around, after establishing our very little knowledge and exhausting our ideas, Ryder and Coya began to bicker amongst themselves. This caused Coya to get upset and ignore the rest of what we had to say, before she eventually fell asleep. Ryder then went quiet as well, leaving me to come up with more ideas by myself.

They have put their trust in me when it comes to all of this crazy unbelievable stuff, and for that I am thankful. I don't want to let them down, not after everything they've been through. I just wish I could figure out an easier way to work together. We're already confined to these cells and have very little mobility or freedom when it comes to speaking to each other. So having them fight when we do speak only makes it that much harder.

I can imagine that it's difficult for them both to get along after being stuck together for so long. But I wish they would just put that aside so we can work together on this. I know that Coya cares for him, I can see it in her eyes and hear it in her voice. She speaks to him like a mother would, and he teases her for it, but it's obvious that he cares for her too.

I glance at Ryder's cell and freeze, startled to see him staring right at me while his fingers fidget with his shirt.

I sit completely frozen. I can't tell how long he's been staring at me, and I can't get myself to look away. My cheeks flush with a rare heat against the usual icy chill. His eyes peer into mine with the same intensity as the day I first saw him. He holds my gaze as though he's searching for something or trying to delve deep within me to figure something out.

A shiver runs through my body but still he holds my gaze, breathing slowly. Being able to actually watch his chest rise and fall with every breath, and see his eyes looking at me unflinchingly as though I weren't able to see him as well. It makes me wonder if he has always stared at me like this before I could see through the dark.

Finally, after moments that feel like an eternity, he breaks the spell with a slight smile, a smile that almost resembles a smirk.

"What are you thinking about?" he whispers through the metal bars that contain him. His voice is an alluring sound that I wish I could hear more and more without any restrictions.

I peel my eyes away, getting my thoughts in order and debating whether I should be honest or not. Quickly an urge tugs at something inside me to be open with him. Something about him makes me want to reveal every part of myself, completely unfiltered. I feel pulled to him in every way.

"I was just thinking about you and Coya," I say as nonchalantly as possible.

He arches an eyebrow, surprised. "What about us?"

"I was just wondering how long you both have been stuck in here together... and how to get you two to stop fighting," I say the last part in a quick mumble.

He chuckles softly and the sound is like sweet music. "Well, that might be hard. We are both really stubborn."

"Obviously..." I mutter. He chuckles once more, but it's short lived. Without warning, his smile disappears, and his face flattens into a blank stare.

"Coya was the first person I met here besides Cock-eye and his *minions*. I was alone for so long until they brought her here when I was just a kid, probably twelve or thirteen."

He pauses as though he's lost himself in a very distant memory. I crawl closer to the bars of my cell to close the space between us.

"Hey?" I say, pulling him back to the present.

He blinks a few times to recollect his thoughts before continuing.

"Before Coya came, I didn't know other people were out there— good people who weren't going to jab me with knives or needles, or leave me in a dark room for days. She took care of me and protected me..." His voice diminishes to below a whisper. "She would sing to me when I was scared... Back then, I was so scared, but she made me feel safe and not alone. We always used to get along..." He trails off.

Tears threaten to escape my eyes. I swallow, working through the bubble in my throat so I can speak.

Hearing his pain is almost unbearable... My assumptions from before were true; they care about each other, but it's so much more than that. All they had was each other... and Ryder was just a kid when she came. I remember how she spoke about the unknown child that she'd lost.

Ryder has been like a child to her.

"What happened? Why don't you get along anymore?" I manage to ask, my voice weak.

His mouth presses into a hard line as his brows pinch together. He doesn't want to say whatever it is that's causing him so much pain, but I have to know.

"What is it?" I insist.

He sighs deeply. "When I escaped, I didn't realize that I would be leaving her behind. It happened so fast, I didn't have time to think about it," he finally says.

I suck in a sharp breath as I begin to understand the gravity of their relationship and everything they've been through together. All of the pain he must have caused her, and himself. I hadn't realized.

When I first woke up here, I knew there was tension between them, and I knew he had escaped before. But it never dawned on me that he had to have escaped without her.

He left her behind.

The thought of myself leaving either of them here makes me sick to my stomach. Now that I know the truth about us, I could never escape without them. But it seems he didn't have much of a choice, from what he's said... At least that is what I want to tell myself. There has to be a reason.

"How did it happen? How did you escape, and why didn't you take her with you?" I ask, glancing over at Coya and seeing her still body sound asleep. She's curled up into a ball, the only comfortable way to sleep here to fight against the cold.

I need to know why he did it and how. Not only because I can't believe he would have left her on purpose, but also because I've been waiting to hear how he escaped in the first place. He's never seemed willing to talk about any of this until now. I hope hearing how he did it might help us escape as well. All of us. *Together.*

He sighs heavily, breaking eye contact with me. He stares down at his shoes, which I can now see are dirty, worn-out black boots. He shifts uncomfortably and combs his long hair back before leaning onto his hands and staring up at the ragged ceiling.

"They were taking me somewhere else. It was the first time I had ever been outside and the first time I had ever been in or even seen a car. They put me in the back of one. Which ended up being a stupid mistake on their part." A small smirk forms on his face but quickly disappears as he continues.

"Seeing the outside for the first time was like nothing I had ever imagined. Coya had tried to describe it to me before, but that was nothing close to the real thing." I savor his words, imagining what it might be like to see the outside world again. I can't remember any specific place, but I can see the image of sunsets in my mind, and imagine the feeling of wind and warmth. When I think of a particular thing like a river, I can almost see an image of it and all of its roaring rapids. Having these images leads me to believe I have been outside once. What I wouldn't give to be outside again...

I try to keep my attention on Ryder as he continues.

"I don't know where they were taking me or why, but I remember it began to rain as they were driving, and I just remember how amazing it was to see it for the first time. But after that my memory gets a bit fuzzy... I started to feel this crazy electricity go through me, and before I knew it, all the men in the car were paralyzed."

My eyes widen. "Paralyzed?"

He nods slowly. "They couldn't move. I didn't know how it happened, but I knew I had to get out of there. And so, I did. I got away," he concludes, his voice full of regret.

I blink back more tears as I imagine everything he went through, all of the pain and confusion. *All of the loneliness.* I knew there was no way he could have left Coya on purpose. He didn't know what else to do.

"You shouldn't blame yourself. It wasn't your fault. You would have taken her with you if you had the chance to and had known what you are capable of," I whisper softly, but loud enough for him to hear the certainty in my voice.

"We still don't know what we're capable of or how to control it—"

"But we will! And when we do, we'll get out of here *together*. I promise," I cut him off, forcing his attention back on me.

He stares into me, his eyes clouding with an emotion I don't recognize. "You know, you're really cute when you get all assertive," he says smoothly.

I quickly look away, a small smile creeping onto my lips.

"Thank you," he says suddenly, his voice sounding more serious. His hand grabs hold of a metal bar as he brings himself closer. "Thank you for talking to me about all of this, and being who you are." His thumb caresses the side of the metal as he leans his forehead against it. It makes me wish that there weren't ten or so feet between us and that like the metal, I could feel his touch.

The room grows quiet except for the soft sounds of our breathing.

CHAPTER 14

Maze

Why am I running?

Someone is chasing me and will kill me once they catch me. They're going to kill us both. I stare down at my hand gripping another as I'm being pulled forward. *But whose hand is it?* I look up to see their face but it's nothing but blurriness.

"They're gaining on us!"

The dream suddenly shifts to darkness then all I see are orange flames, bearded dragons, and soft brown eyes.

***

I'm awakened gently by the light seeping in from between the curtains that hang in the window. I lift myself, ignoring every slight ache begging me not to. I try to wrap my head around everything that happened the day before. The memories from yesterday are crystal clear, but everything before then is still a blank.

Rubbing the sleep out of my eyes, I try once again to think back as hard as I can but there's nothing. It's completely black, and after giving myself a small headache, I decide to give it a rest for now.

The memory of Ryder floods my mind making my heart flutter. I can't help but feel excited for whatever he has in store for us today and am just as excited to see him again.

Jeez, what am I, a hopeless romantic?

I lift the blanket off myself and as soon as I do so, I'm struck with horror at the sight before me. Blood covers my legs and is soaked through to the mattress.

My hands begin shaking as I lift myself cautiously off the bed, hoping not to drip anywhere else. I fear that I must be hurt somewhere for a moment, but the realization quickly hits me.

This is the worst, most embarrassing thing that could have happened. After everything Ryder has done for me, letting me sleep in his bed, I had to go and bleed all over it! *This is a nightmare.*

I wrap the blanket around my waist and quietly step out of the van, hoping he's still asleep. I don't even look in the direction he's in as I run to the bathroom and shut the door behind me.

After I pee, I scrub the boxers with toilet paper but with no luck. They're stained beyond saving. I soak some more with water and clean the blood off my legs, then wrap as much of it as I can around my hand, creating a makeshift pad and hoping it'll hold me over until I can figure something out. *God, why did I have to start my period now?*

I shamefully open the bathroom door, gripping the blanket tightly around me as I waddle back toward the campsite. Ryder is awake and staring out at the water but turns around as he hears me approach. "Good morning, sleepy head!" he chimes.

Jeez, he sure is chipper in the morning...

I sheepishly sit down, working up the courage to explain to him what happened. "Morning," I grumble.

"How'd you sleep?" He eyes the blanket I have wrapped around me.

"Well, I slept fine. It was kind of cold last night but..." I trail off, trudging my way to the point. "But this morning kind of sucked because I woke up in a puddle of blood all over your bed, because I started my period," I finally rush out, afraid to look up at him.

"Shit, I'm so sorry Rainy. Don't worry about it. We can drive down to the convenience store and pick you up some tampons or whatever else you need, okay? And don't worry about the bed. I'll clean it up later." He sets his hand down on my knee in an attempt to comfort me.

"You're not upset or anything?"

He frowns. "Why would I be upset? It's normal." A reassuring smile forms on his mouth. "Seriously, don't worry about it, okay? Just let me know if there's anything I can do for you."

I set my hand down on top of his, and emotion starts to overcome me as the feeling of embarrassment dissipates. "Thank you. I don't know where I'd be right now if I hadn't met you."

He removes his hand from my knee to pick a small stick from my hair and flicks it away. I have to force myself not to shiver at the gentle gesture.

"I'm happy to help," he says.

***

We drive to the nearest convenience store a couple of miles out. As soon as we pull into the parking spot, I become hyper aware that I'm dressed in oversized men's clothing... stained with blood. I'm mortified by the thought of asking him to grab what I need, but I'm even more scared to go in myself. Ryder seems to read my mind once again because he says, "Will any tampons work? Is there anything else I can grab for you?"

My breathing shallows as I try to compose myself. "Um, I'm not sure... regular should be fine. Thank you."

He opens the door to hop out. "Don't mention it!" He smiles that big smile of his before proceeding to the store.

This whole experience has wreaked havoc on my nerves. I know Ryder says he's fine about the whole thing, and I don't doubt him, but it has made my situation even more unpredictable. If I had remembered who I was then I would have known that my period was about to start and would have been prepared for it. All of this is just another gruesome reminder that this is my reality, the unknown and unpredictable.

Despite everything though, I couldn't be more thankful to have met someone like Ryder. The thought is overwhelming. I feel guilty for having thought he was just some weirdo. A cute weirdo, but that's besides the point.

A few minutes pass and I start to wonder what's taking him so long. Maybe he got confused and doesn't know which ones to buy? Soon I'm filled with guilt once more. I try to distract myself with music on the radio and picking the dirt from under my fingernails, but still the worry lingers. After a few minutes pass, I can't ignore it any longer and just as I prepare myself to get out, he strolls outside with two big grocery bags in both hands. I push open the car door for him as he struggles to get inside and sit down, setting the bags in front of me.

"Sorry I took so long. I grabbed a couple of different options for you just in case. Plus, they had clothes in there so I grabbed a few t-shirts and shorts for ya."

I peek inside the bags at all the goodies and rummage around the different colored t-shirts and cotton fabric shorts. "Thank you so much. This is more than enough." I fight the urge to fling my arms around him.

"Oh, there's also a little surprise for you in there as well."

I dig inside the bag until I find a large chocolate bar at the bottom. I'm almost giddy with excitement, the sudden craving making my mouth water. "But why?"

He flashes me a wide smile, his eyes shining with pride. "I heard that chocolate can help make girls feel better when they're on their.. er, *cycle* you know, so I figured I'd give it a try. I'm happy to see that it worked."

"That's usually after they've already eaten it." I nudge him playfully as I open it and take a bite.

He shrugs, his grin heart-stopping. "Still worked."

I glance inside the second bag as we make our way back to the campsite.

"Oh yeah, I also grabbed a toothbrush, hairbrush, and other things you might need," he explains nonchalantly.

I stare at the items, feeling on the brink of spoiled. "Don't worry, I'll repay you for all of this. You've done so much for me already."

"I've already thought all about it. You can come with me to work on the farm. It'll make my job easier and more fun."

"I thought you said you didn't have a job?" I eye him curiously. It dawns on me that I haven't given much thought to how Ryder affords everything he buys.

"Well, I don't. It's more of an odd job that I do for a friend. Don't worry, I'll take you there soon and you'll understand."

We make it back to the campsite and I rush to the bathroom to quickly change into a new pair of clothes, feeling much more secure now with an actual tampon.

I slip on the tight navy-blue V-neck and the soft cotton black shorts, and bask in the comfort they bring me. I check myself in the mirror, careful to avoid the thoughts from the day before.

My hair sits in a curly mess with large knots forming. *Jeez, did I not take care of myself?*

I try to play with it and make it look halfway decent with the brush. After some time, I manage to brush the knots out and relax the curls with some water. I sigh. It will have to do for now. I check out my teeth and the slight yellow tint they have from the chocolate and not being cleaned for who knows how long. I take the toothbrush and toothpaste and happily brush them, feeling instant relief to have clean teeth and I'm sure, much better smelling breath.

I give myself one last look over in the small mirror. My body is thin and sort of awkward looking, my face is well... my face. It's hard for me to form an opinion of myself and how I look, because I hardly know this person but somehow, this person is me... This is gonna take a lot of getting used to.

I walk back to the campsite and Ryder already has water and sandwiches waiting for us. "Wow, you look great! How do you feel?" He beams.

I rub my arm, feeling an odd sense of shyness take over when he looks at me. "I feel much better now, thank you." I play with the turkey sandwich in my hand and try to fight a blush.

"Good. As long as you're happy, I'm happy," he manages to say through a mouth full of food.

I shake my head, rolling my eyes. "You gotta stop talking with your mouth full! You're gonna choke."

He laughs, his cheeks full and resembling a chipmunk before he swallows and they deflate. "Sorry, I'm still getting used to having a lady around. I'll try to remember my manners." He winks and I smile at the sight of it. It's starting to become my favorite mental image of him.

CHAPTER 15

Rainy

The piercing sound of buttons beeping fills the room like nails on a chalkboard. It is a sound that I both fear and hope for, because it could either mean the beginning of horrible unknown experiments or the end of countless days of starvation. I just hope for the latter.

I close my eyes tightly, praying to the unknown source of life. Perhaps God, or perhaps the voices from the In Between— anyone who might listen. *Please let it be food... Please. Please. Please.*

The squeaking of my cell door opening causes my eyelids to flutter open. Three towering orange figures stand before me, anticipating my next move.

Damn, looks like my prayers weren't answered today.

I timidly stand up, careful not to make any sudden movements. They watch me carefully, obviously worried I might try to *warp* again or something else to try and escape. After inspecting me, they cover my head with a bag much like before and detach the tube from my back. Its absence gives me instant relief from its stabbing sensation, a relief I hadn't noticed when they had taken me before because of the fear and chaos happening within and around me.

"Don't put that bullshit over my head! I can walk myself, fuckers." Ryder's voice spits from behind me as they walk me out of my cell. It brings me a small comfort, knowing that I'm not being taken alone, and that he'll be right behind me. I try to listen for any indication of Coya being taken as well, but I can't hear anything over the sound of Ryder continuing to resist and mock the orange suits at my back. I don't understand why he tries so hard to instigate them. What is he trying to prove? Does he like being punished?

They sit me down and remove the bag from my head. I could already tell where we were from the moment I felt the warmth emitting from the intense surrounding light. I hug myself, allowing the warmth and clean air to soothe me. Everything about this small room is the complete opposite from the one we're always trapped in. This room offers everything that that room doesn't, and it's hard not to appreciate every bit of it.

I glance around the closed-in brightly lit space. Ryder is sitting in front of me like before and I expect to see Coya right by my side as well, but she isn't. It's just me and Ryder, alone.

"Where's Coya? Why isn't she here?" I ask him, failing to hide the panic building in my voice.

"I don't know. They usually always bring her," he answers, speaking mostly out loud to himself as his eyes dart around.

I suck in my breath. "Why wouldn't they bring her now? Are they going to hurt her?!" My voice chokes with more panic as tears blur my vision, and I imagine what horrible things they might do to her. I can't stop myself from remembering all the stories they've told me in the past, about the people who have come before me and how they were most likely killed. I can't stop myself from thinking that could be happening to Coya right at this very moment.

My body begins to shake involuntarily.

Ryder leans forward, forcing my attention on him and away from all of my intrusive thoughts. I hold my breath as I take in the sight of him, only inches away from my face, close enough to touch with no barriers separating us.

"Listen to me. We have to stay calm, okay?" He speaks gently, instantly calming me with the sound of his voice. "They would never hurt her. She's too important to them, remember?" he says the last part in a hushed whisper. I nod my head and wipe away the lingering tears from my cheeks.

He stays leaning forward, that same distant look returning to his eyes. I sit still, not daring to move or break eye contact. A tingly warmth spreads through me underneath his gaze. It's a warmth almost comparable to what I felt in the In Between. An otherworldly sensation that I never want to end.

The room is silent. If only whatever this is could last forever... His eyes on me, the tickle of his breath brushing against my skin, this unnatural pull threading between us.

Slowly, he lifts his hand and traces the tips of his fingers down my forehead to my chin.

My body turns to jelly the moment I feel his touch. A touch that I have yearned for from the moment I saw him after I woke up in this place— which seems like a lifetime ago now. I lean into him, everything else melting away. All of the fears from before disappear and are replaced by this euphoric sensation that tingles throughout my entire body, beginning at my head and dripping down my back to my stomach. A feeling I've definitely only ever felt at the In Between, something so indescribable and familiar. Something that feels like *home.*

I could get lost in this forever. *I could get lost in him.*

Suddenly the wall to my side shifts and opens, bringing me back to a cruel reality.

"No touching!" Cock-eye storms in, his one loose eye swinging downwards like a pocket-watch; swaying back and forth to hypnotize its victims.

Ryder pulls away and we instantly sit back as far away from each other as possible. Ryder straightens his back, his whole demeanor changing completely with Cock-eye in the room. He doesn't act as careless as he does when he's around the orange suits, but is more obedient and fearful.

"Grab them both," Cock-eye commands the orange suits standing by his side. They immediately obey, grabbing us by our arms and pulling us to our feet. They force us out of the soothing warm room and through to the other side of the wall.

On the other side, we appear to be in the same chemical-smelling room as before. The orange suits sit us down on medical beds beside each other before disappearing into the walls again, leaving us alone with Cock-eye and all of his terrifying metal devices.

My mouth goes dry as my eyes scan everywhere, remembering the chilling events that took place the last time I was in here. I hate everything about this room and Cock-eye. I would rather be anywhere else but here.

I glance over at Ryder, hoping to gain some of his usual strength, but his eyes are elsewhere. He glares ahead at Cock-eye. I can't get his attention, but still a sense of comfort washes over me at the fact that he's here with me now, and that I'm not stuck here alone. *But I'd feel even better if Coya were here too. To know she's at least okay... alive.*

Cock-eye paces the room, jotting things down on his notepad as he mumbles incoherently to himself in the neurotic way that he's done before. He does this for a while, not looking in our direction even once. It's as if we're not even in the same room as him and he's in his own little world completely separate from ours.

After sitting like this for God knows how long and watching him pace back and forth, the anticipation causes anger to build up inside me that quickly replaces almost all of the fear.

"Where is Atlacoya?" My voice interrupts his chaotic rambling, surprising me by how stern and confident it sounds compared to how I actually feel.

He stops his pacing, his eyes still focused on the notepad. "Atlacoya... Atlacoya..." he repeats to himself. "Goddess of drought and barren land." A raspy chuckle escapes his throat as if he's just heard a humorous inside-joke.

I bite my tongue hard enough to taste blood, fighting the urge to yell, scream, and demand an answer. I know that it wouldn't do any good and wouldn't get me anywhere with him and his insanity.

"Do you know what is required for all life?" Cock-eye's voice changes completely, sounding flat and serious. It sends chills throughout my entire body. He's looking at me now, his face emotionless and waiting for a response.

I shake my head, not wanting to risk angering him and getting a repeat of last time. He turns his attention to Ryder and waits for an answer. His jaw tightens and relaxes before he reluctantly shakes his head.

"The one vital element that all life requires, that each planet must have for life to evolve and flourish, is water. Without water, nothing could exist. Water is the true source of life... The source of power and energy." Cock-eye drones and pauses to see our expressions, almost as if he's testing to see how we'll react to what he's saying.

What is he going on about?

I breathe slowly, not fully understanding his words but trying to connect them to what we already know.

"But life is fragile and temporary, like most things. Power and energy, however, are not," he says the last part in a low dark tone as he turns to a table and rummages through the different devices. Something about the way he finishes his sentence prickles my skin with goosebumps.

Once he finds what he's looking for, he turns to face me. His hand grips a large needle and syringe with vibrant light blue liquid inside. He walks to my side, each menacing step causing his crooked eye to jerk. He forcefully grabs hold of my arm. The touch of his skin is cold and clammy like wet clay, yet rough and demanding.

"Now this may hurt a lot, but I can promise you one thing, it won't matter in the very grand scheme of things. No one can hear you; no one can help you. But not to worry, little bug. Your useless counterpart will be here to watch." His cheeks spread into a wide toothy grin that causes my blood to run cold.

"No, please don't," I beg as I try to free my arm from his grasp. He tightens his grip around me, making it impossible to break away. The evil look in his eye and the echo of his words frighten me to my core. I don't want to feel what horribly excruciating pain this unknown liquid might inflict. I almost give up hope, accepting my fate as the needle reaches my arm.

The air shifts, and everything starts to move in slow motion all around me.

"Don't touch her!" Ryder yells and his voice seems to make the entire room vibrate and shake violently. Within a second, he's standing and grabs Cock-eye by his arm, ripping him away from me with force.

"You're not gonna fucking hurt her!" He screams into his face. Ryder's eyes fill with an intense hatred. It's a look threatening enough to make even me flinch.

My heart leaps out of my chest. I hold my breath, expecting to see Cock-eye fight back or summon the orange suits back to punish us, but he doesn't. The room stops shaking and everything falls silent.

Cock-eye's body contorts, making a disgusting crunching sound before he stands completely frozen. His arms are curled to his chest and his legs are glued to the floor in a buckled stance.

"You useless bastard— I should kill you both! You disgusting, pitiful lifeform!" Cock-eye gasps through gritted teeth, unable to move. His lengthy body is shaking beneath its own weight, threatening to collapse in on itself.

An instant later the walls from where we emerged shift and a group of orange suits come rushing in. Within a second, one jabs a long black stick into Ryder's side, creating a painful zapping noise. Ryder falls to his knees as two others grab and drag him away.

I try to scream for him and rush forward, but am too late. An Orange suit covers my mouth with fabric the moment I take a breath. Immediately my body grows fuzzy and everything begins to melt away as I feel them drag me away from the medical bed and out of the room.

"Take them back. We'll find a better enclosure for them and take more precautions. They know the truth now; we can't let them harness it. Inject the Visors, we'll keep them weak for the time being." Cock-eye's voice echoes from behind me as they drag me away. I try to stay conscious but my body quickly becomes numb with each inhale. The last thing I feel is a sharp stab in my neck before everything fades away.

CHAPTER 16

Maze

We spend the day by the water, dipping our feet in occasionally as Ryder tells me more of the crazy adventures he's had. He tells me about how he once traveled to Colorado to a festival filled with amazing art and people. And how everyone would stay up all hours of the night, taking different hallucinogens and dancing until they collapsed.

I imagine the stories as he tells them. A slight feeling of envy takes over me as I start to picture myself being there, experiencing all of it with him. He tells me about how once he got pulled over in California and the cop was such an asshole that Dude bit him on the leg. They had to make a run for it, and he was so surprised that they actually got away.

I watch in awe as he tells me story after story. Part of me wants to ask what his life was like before he was a traveler, but I decide against it, because something tells me it would change the entire mood. I don't want to do anything that might cause that big smile of his to disappear.

Once the sun begins to set, we get back into the van and set out for Ryder's 'favorite lookout.' He's been talking about it nonstop since I've met him and ever since we got in the van his body is shaky and he's grinning even more so than usual.

I can feel his excitement the closer we get to it, and am also becoming more anxious to see it.

We head up a winding desert road as we scale a large mountain. I stare out the window with anticipation, unsure of what I might see but excited regardless.

It's dark when Ryder finally pulls over to the side of the road in a nonexistent parking spot. I try to see past the darkness, but from what I can tell there is nothing for miles as I look out to the flat land below us.

"From here we have to walk," he says as he grabs a portable lamp from the back of the van.

He leads me up an inconspicuous trail, and my stomach swarms with a feeling I can't recognize. I try to keep my eyes on our feet where the light illuminates the ground.

We climb for a few minutes and I start to feel a bit light-headed by the excursion, but soon we finally arrive at the top.

Ryder turns off the lamp and I have to blink hard a few times to let my eyes re-adjust. "What do you think? Isn't it beautiful?" He waves his arms up to the dark heavens surrounding us. I can barely make out the outline of his body against the many twinkling lights.

The night sky is even grander from where we're standing than it was back at the campsite. It spreads out infinitely, hugging the earth below it.

I hold my breath as I take in the vast number of stars hanging above us. I almost have to force myself not to reach up in an attempt to touch them.

I can't tell if I'm breathless from the climb or the sheer beauty in front of me. My eyes trace along the pattern of the stars' pattern, until they catch blurry twinkling lights near the horizon. I squint hard to try and make out the shapes but it's useless against the distance.

"What's over there?" I point toward them as Ryder walks over to stand beside me.

"Oh, that's Vegas. It's a disappointing excuse for a city. A complete hellhole." For the first time since I met him, there is honest dislike and almost resentment in his voice.

"Why's that?"

"Because it sucks the life out of people," he says, dismissing it. I decide not to poke at him for more details, not wanting to spoil our time here.

We sit down side by side in a silent agreement to enjoy the moment.

"It's so weird, I feel like I've been here before," I finally say, breaking the silence as I lay down to take in the sky.

Ryder peers down at me, his eyes flashing an unnatural glow in the darkness. I look away, I figure the dark must be playing tricks on me. "I felt the same way when I first came here," he says it so close I can faintly feel his breath against my skin.

I stare ahead, focusing on how to breathe right. *Not too much... and not too little.*

He lays down, the side of his body slightly brushing against mine, creating an electric rush that shoots through my skin.

My heart rate is increasing, and I just hope for the life of me that he can't hear it. I try to focus on the stars laying over us, but his warmth against me makes it almost impossible.

I don't understand what's come over me. These last couple of days have almost felt like a lifetime, *probably because it has been a lifetime for me.* But every moment I spend with him, feelings I don't understand become harder to ignore and this odd familiar feeling becomes more frequent, nagging at my insides. *Are these feelings normal?*

Ryder points to a shooting star above us as it streaks across the sky. "That was a big one!" I can feel him smiling beside me and I'm thankful for the distraction.

"I see why this is your favorite lookout spot."

He perches himself up on his elbows. "It's definitely one of the most beautiful spots on this planet." He stares down at me and it's hard to make out his face in the darkness but I can feel his gaze burning into me.

I quickly feel vulnerable laying down with his eyes on me, so I sit up as well and look away. *Get a hold of yourself.*

"If you could go anywhere in the world, where would you go?" he asks, looking off into a different direction now.

I think hard for a moment as I stare at the back of him. "I'm not sure, I haven't really thought about it." *I wonder where my old self would have wanted to go.*

"Do you remember the different places that exist?"

I narrow my eyes on him. "Of course, I do! I'm not brain-dead. I just can't remember who I am or what I would have wanted," I snap, annoyed by the question but mostly annoyed with myself.

"Sorry, I didn't mean it like that. I'm still just trying to understand what it is you can and can't remember," he mutters with remorse and I instantly regret lashing out at him. It wasn't meant to be directed toward him, but more so my circumstances.

"No, I'm sorry. I'm still trying to figure it out myself. I just get frustrated when I try to think about it, and I can't remember all the things about myself."

He lays his hand on top of mine, shocking me with that same electricity as it shivers up my spine. I can't move. I'm afraid if I do, he'll stop touching me.

"Maybe instead of trying to figure out what you would have wanted before losing your memory, try to think about what it is you want now, and build new memories and wants for who you are *now*," he says softly, his voice drifting to me with warmth and understanding.

I hadn't thought about that before. This whole time I have been trying to figure out everything my old self liked and would have wanted. Desperately searching for who that person is, but maybe that person doesn't exist anymore... Perhaps I should try to move on and learn who I am now. *Who's to say if I'll ever regain those memories again.*

I exhale deeply and it feels as though a large burden has been lifted from my shoulders.

"Have you ever seen the Northern lights?" I finally ask. He shakes his head in response, his body now stiff with intrigue. "I think I would want to see them." I nod as if in agreement with myself. The thought of seeing colorful waves in the sky brings a yearning to my heart that I've never felt before.

"Then that's where we'll go. We'll find the Northern lights." His voice grows louder with excitement.

I laugh in disbelief. "How? Where would we even go?"

He squeezes my hand, determined. "Alaska of course! It's perfect! I've never been and it would be the perfect adventure."

The idea seems crazy and out of reach but his determination squashes all my doubts. "Okay, let's do it," I say, not allowing myself a second to question it.

"Okay?" He beams. Standing up, he pulls me into his arms and swings me around effortlessly.

I don't realize until after he sets me down that I'm giggling like a child.

"Tomorrow we'll go to the farm and start working to save money for the trip," he begins, planning out loud. "I can't wait for you to meet Richard, he's a hell of a guy."

***

We make our way back to the van and I'm practically floating with this new-found ambition for the future. I could almost float away if it weren't for Ryder's hand in mine, anchoring my feet to the ground.

Before now everything felt so uncertain and pointless. But because of him, I now have something to look forward to, to strive for. I didn't think I would ever find a future so bright. I didn't allow myself to give my future much thought at all.

We arrive back at the van and Ryder begins rummaging around inside. "We'll camp here tonight then leave early in the morning for the farm," he explains as he pulls out his sleeping bag.

"Uh, actually, I was kinda hoping you would sleep with me inside the van tonight," I blurt out before I can stop myself.

He pauses and studies me for a moment. "Are you sure? I really don't mind sleeping outside."

My cheeks turn hot. "Well, it was pretty chilly last night and I just thought it would be better if you were there... I really don't mind," I ramble on.

"Ah I see. You wanna keep each other *warm*." He smirks, wiggling his eyebrows.

"Not like that! Don't get any ideas." I roll my eyes and storm into the van.

I slide onto the bed and under the covers and am stunned to find it already replaced with a fresh new set of sheets. I don't know when he would have had time to replace them but I try not to think about it.

He gets in next to me and we're soon laying side by side.

It's quiet except for the soft sounds of our breathing and the crickets chirping from outside. Each nerve in my body is on high alert but I try to relax them and close my eyes.

I think I might fall asleep for a moment until Ryder stirs, turning to face me and draping his arm over me.

My eyelids fly open and I don't know how to react at first. Without thinking I follow suit, facing him and meeting his eyes. He smiles slightly, his face filled with a look almost resembling longing, but I can't be sure.

"Goodnight, Rainy," he whispers before closing his eyes.

The humming of my heartbeat grows as loud as the crickets outside as I study his relaxed face lit up by the soft moonlight peeking in through the window. I resist the urge to inch closer to him, to feel his skin against my lips and wrap my arms around him, pulling his body close to mine.

Jesus, I really don't know what the hell's wrong with me.

I force my eyes shut and try to relax my anxious heartbeat again. *Of all its aching desires...* I barely know the guy, but all I want is to get closer to him somehow.

This is going to be a long night.

CHAPTER 17

Rainy

"Where is she?! What did you do with her!" I scream at the top of my lungs. My voice is hoarse and my throat sore from screaming and yelling for I don't know how long. Long enough for my lips to crack and bleed from dehydration, and my spirit to threaten to break as my body trembles with weakness.

When I woke up, I found myself back on my cell's cold, hard floor. Coya was gone and the tube was no longer attached to my back. I've screamed for what feels like days in hopes of getting the orange suits' attention and getting answers from them.

So far, nothing.

A sick feeling in my gut has grown harder to ignore with each passing second. I can't let them hurt Coya, the thought puts me in a spiral where all I can do is scream and cry, but it hasn't made any difference.

Not knowing what happened to her or if she's even still alive... It's tearing me apart.

"Rainy, look at me." Ryder's soft but commanding voice brings my gaze forward, reluctantly. I stare at him through the metal bars as I try to settle my wavering breath against silent sobs. "It's gonna be okay. I want you to try something. Take a deep breath in from your mouth, hold it for four seconds and blow it out your nose. Okay? Can you do that?"

I shake my head, making more tears fall away. "Why?"

"Just do it with me. Okay, ready?" He inhales deeply into his mouth while holding up four fingers for me to see, putting one down as each second passes. I try to suck in air, watching him carefully as I do so, before blowing it out when all of his fingers are down.

"Good, again."

I follow his lead, swallowing more gulps of air and holding it in. My head grows lighter with each passing second. My heart rate slows and the heavy feeling in my stomach seems to dissipate slightly.

"There now, you see? It's gonna be okay. We have to stay calm and think clearly through this. For all we know, they could have just moved her to a new place, same as they tried to do with me before I escaped. Hell, maybe she even managed to escape too. Either way, jumping to the worst-case scenario is not gonna help us." He pauses, gauging my expression. "We need to stay strong and keep them from thinking they've broken us. Do you understand?"

As I digest his words, a sudden burst of calm fills me. The same sense of calm that seems to only wash over me when he speaks to me this way. An unnatural force that soothes and encourages me more than anything else. *As though he willed it to happen...*

For a moment I can finally feel my muscles relax for the first time in a very long time. I slump back against the wall and nod my head. "Thank you," I try to say but it only comes out in a weak whisper. I try to clear my throat but the harsh dryness doesn't budge.

The room falls silent. My thoughts wander back to the horrible chemical-smelling room and everything that played out before I lost consciousness. All of the fear, anger, and the immense amount of power that leaked through Ryder's fingertips when he grabbed Cock-eye, causing the entire room to shake. I had never seen anything like it. He was willing to kill him, *for me.* The thought spreads warmth deep inside me, until I remember the look in Ryder's eyes. They were chilling. They were no longer the soft honey brown that carried kindness and mischief. They were dark and hateful, capable of unimaginable things. It's hard to imagine Ryder that way. I almost want to believe that I was seeing things, but I know that isn't true.

There wasn't a single ounce of fear in him like I had seen all of the times before when Cock-eye was around. It makes me wonder what changed. What made him so willing to stand up to him now? And what will Cock-eye do now that he's fought back? Chills run down my spine.

"Are you scared of Cock-eye? Do you think he'd hurt us after everything we've done?" I ask, fighting off another shiver.

Ryder stares at the ground, picking at the rubber from the bottom of his black boots. "I won't let him," he says firmly.

I swallow. *Something has changed.* I believe him but part of me fills with doubt nonetheless. "We don't know what he's capable of—"

"I do!" he shouts, making me flinch.

He frowns, his eyes filling with instant regret. He runs his fingers through his hair and turns away. "He needs us. I know that now. Before, he did scare me, yes. He did things to me that I will never be able to forget— even if the memory loss still worked on me, which I wish it would so I *could* forget. That would make things so much easier." He sighs, struggling to find the right words.

"I used to be scared... But after I saw him almost hurt you, I–" His fists tighten at his sides and I can almost feel the anger seeping off of him from where I sit. "Just know that I will never let him touch you again. I will always protect you; I promise." His eyes meet mine again.

I suppress heat from returning to my cheeks as my heart flutters with every wave of emotion. This is more than just a connection we have because of who we are... So much more. Ryder has made me feel things beyond anything else. Things you would never expect to feel in a dark cell that offers nothing more than pain, fear, and hunger. It's a welcomed distraction from all the torment we must endure here. But it also makes it that much harder to be caged only a few feet away from each other, just out of arm's reach.

He tears his eyes away from me as though he can't stand to torture himself with it any longer. "If he wanted to kill us, he would have by now. I don't know why, but *he needs us.*" He emphasizes the last three words, allowing me to take in the true power that they hold. *He needs us.*

Ryder is right. If he had wanted to, he would have. Not just if he wanted to, but if he could... Especially after Ryder has already escaped once and we have both caused so much trouble since I've been here. Hell, Cock-eye said he wanted to do it himself. But he hasn't. This could only mean that no matter what we do, he needs to keep us alive. The only question is, why?

I know he wants us for power, or at least some form of it. But *how* is he using us for power? Why doesn't he just look for others instead of holding onto us? None of it makes any sense.

I lay down on the hard floor, grimacing as the cold pierces into my back before finally growing accustomed to it. At least now, I can finally lay on my back, a luxury I didn't have when the tube was attached to it. And yet, another mystery I don't understand... Why didn't they reattach it? Especially considering everything that's happened.

I dissect each thought as it comes and goes. Someway, somehow, we need to escape. The sooner the better, before anything happens to Coya... *If it hasn't already.*

No. I cannot give in to those thoughts. We will get out of here. All of us. We had all promised to escape together and that we would find her child when we did. And that's exactly what we'll do. I could never live with myself if that didn't happen, if I couldn't find a way. What would be the point of all of this? All of this suffering?

We. Will. Escape. We just have to.

Curling to my side, I try to clear my mind of all of its painful thoughts and do the breathing trick again and again to try and relax. I breathe deeply, counting in my mind for four seconds before exhaling through my nose. Immediately, my mind clears and melts into a fuzzy calm.

It's amazing how quickly it works.

"Where did you learn how to do that breathing trick?" I ask out loud.

"Coya taught me how to do it when I was younger. She would always do it with me when I was scared, which always seemed to calm me down." I can hear the hurt in his voice as he speaks about her. He's just as worried about her as I am, even if he doesn't show it as much.

I quickly try to change the subject to something lighter.

"What was it like outside when you escaped?"

"What do you mean?"

"I mean, what did it look like? Where did you go? I want to know what it was like. I want to hear everything." I try not to sound as desperate as I feel as the questions spew from my lips.

"It was..." He trails off for a moment. "It was bright, dry, and hot as hell at first. Above us is a huge desert that goes on forever, and a world where some people are kind and others, not so much."

"Right above us? You mean that we're underground?"

He nods. "From what I could tell, we're in a facility deep underground."

My insides turn hollow with fear. I suddenly feel closed in, claustrophobic in a way I've never felt before. I hadn't thought too much about where we could be, but I had never thought of the possibility of being underground. It's absolutely terrifying, making the prospect of escaping seem that much farther away.

I do the breathing trick again, over and over until I start to feel light-headed, and the dizziness is all I can think about.

"Tell me more," I blurt, trying to distract myself.

"More? What else do you want to know?"

"Was the food good?" I ask without thinking, as if my stomach has taken control of my mouth and words.

He lets out a laugh, a beautiful sound that washes almost all of the fear away. I'm thankful that the one good thing that has come out of this is being able to speak to each other freely, loudly and openly without the fear of the orange suits coming to punish us. They have made no indication of coming to stop us, my earlier screaming has since proved that.

I bask in the sound of his laugh. I almost have to stop myself from asking him to do it again.

"Oh yeah. The food is amazing up there. The big sandwiches, greasy burgers, and don't even get me started on the chili." He toys with his words, making each thing sound better than the last. My stomach twists up and my mouth instantly fills with saliva, coating my dry throat.

"Okay, okay I get it!" I beg him to stop playfully, but truthfully, I can't stand to hear any more of it. I force my stomach to settle and drag my mind to my earlier questions to distract myself from the gnawing hunger pains. "Where was your favorite place out there?"

He ponders my words as he manages to pull the piece of rubber from his boot he's been picking at. "There was a place I found; it was so incredible— it looked like it was on a completely different planet. At the top of this mountain, you could see so many stars and sometimes even the Milky way galaxy. There was nowhere else like it." His face lights up as he describes it to me and with each detail he shares, my heart swells and mourns for a place I've never been.

At some point as we speak, our hands gravitate toward each other. They now reach out of our cells as far as the metal bars will allow. We rest them against the cold concrete, only a few inches of space separating our fingers from each other.

He continues telling story after story of each beautiful place he witnessed when he was free. Some sound more pleasant than others, but all of them sound like paradise compared to here.

I allow myself to soak in every sweet detail of all the stories he shares, and I let them carry me far away from this place.

CHAPTER 18

Maze

I yawn as I sit in the van's passenger seat, waiting for Ryder to return from the gas station with our coffees. He insisted on us waking up and leaving at dawn. I couldn't argue even though I wish I had. I'm quickly learning that I am definitely not a morning person.

I rub the grogginess from my eyes when Ryder returns and hands me a coffee. His fingers brush against mine, returning my mind to this morning when I woke up and found myself sprawled across his chest. I chug the hot liquid down, trying hard to push away the memory.

"Is the coffee alright?" He arches an eyebrow, inspecting the flushed look on my face.

I nod, recollecting my thoughts. "Yes, thank you! I'm still just trying to wake up." I try to sound normal but fail miserably.

A knowing smile tugs on his lips. "Hopefully the coffee will help. We have a long drive today. It'll take a few hours before we get to the farm."

I slouch back into the seat as he begins driving.

Time drags on. I watch out the window as the earth flies by, searching for something interesting to talk about. *Something the person I am now would think of.*

Eventually, I give up. I divert my energy to the radio, the muffled music cutting in and out.

"What's your favorite kind of music?" I blurt.

Ryder gives me a surprised look then thinks for a moment. "Tough to say. I love any kind of music that makes me feel good. Sometimes it depends on the experience I'm having or sometimes I like music that reminds me of an experience I've already had."

I lean back, impatient and not completely satisfied by his answer. He always seems to give me these long and complicated responses that always leave me with more questions than answers.

I chew on my cheek and decide that this time I will get a real answer from him. "Okay then, what's your favorite song?"

"My favorite song?" he repeats to himself.

"Yeah, like a song you've loved since you were a kid," I elaborate.

He tenses his shoulders as if he's uncomfortable thinking that far back and shakes his head. "I don't have a favorite song."

I find that really hard to believe. I may not remember mine, but that doesn't give him an excuse not to have one.

I purse my lips, suddenly intrigued and unwilling to give up on my mission. "Well, well. Look who's the one full of mystery now," I say with exasperation.

He shrugs. "What can I say? I'm a man of many secrets."

I sigh dramatically at his sarcasm. Thinking for a moment, I look for a change of topic that might reveal more about him. "So, what was your life like before you were a traveler?" I finally ask, letting my curiosity get the best of me.

His fingers grip the steering wheel and he glues his eyes to the road. It's clear the question has brought about emotions he's not yet ready to disclose.

"I'm sorry. You don't have to answer that." I knew I shouldn't have asked. I don't know why I decided now was a good time to ignore my instincts, they're all I really have.

He shakes his head again but doesn't take his eyes off the road.

"It's fine. I just usually try not to think too much about that time in my life. There were a lot of things that happened that I have tried to run away from. It's the reason I live my life the way I do now. Everything is my choice."

I hold my tongue, forcing myself not to ask him for more explanation. I wish there was some way I could get more details out of him, but I know that my efforts would be futile. All I really want is to learn who he is, inside and out. The good and the bad. *Maybe someday...*

"Anyway, what matters is the here and now. Living life in the moment." He forces a smile but it doesn't quite reach his eyes.

His words bounce around my head. *Something from his past that he's trying to run away from.* I feel that something must have really hurt him for him to have decided to completely remove himself from the outside world and live on the road. The thought of it tugs on my heart and I wish I could do or say more that might help him. The same way he has helped me.

"We're almost there." He interrupts my thoughts. "It should only be a few more minutes." His voice is back to being lighthearted.

We pull off of the main highway and onto a long unmaintained dirt road. We drive it for only a little while, but the bumpiness makes it feel like forever. It eventually leads to a massive plastic-covered greenhouse. The greenhouse is the first thing that catches my eye because everything else dwarfs in comparison. The plastic is an off-white color and I cannot see what's inside of it.

Alongside the greenhouse is a one-story brick house with an old barn that sits beside it. There are miles of flat desert land on either side of the farm. Long straw-like grass grows in scattered patches as we pull up. Behind everything is a large ridged hill that casts a shadow over all the structures. From what I can tell, the farm is isolated with nothing else around it as far as the eye can see. I'm guessing it would have been impossible for anyone to find if they didn't know exactly where to look.

"Where are all the farm animals?" I glance around, confused by the lack of them.

"It's not that kind of farm." He gives me a sheepish look but before I can ask more, a tall man walks from the barn toward the van.

We both get out and soon Ryder is clasping the man's shoulders and pulling him in for a hug. The man doesn't seem particularly pleased by the embrace but does nothing to pull away from it.

"Richard! It's been too long, my man!" Ryder beams as he speaks to him.

"It's only been a year, Ryder. Get yourself together." The man grumbles back, his face set sternly, but I can almost see a small hint of amusement. "You should have told me you were coming. I was getting ready to grab my gun seeing a van pulling in I didn't recognize."

"Sorry about that. It's new."

They speak to each other back and forth as they catch up while I stand back awkwardly, not wanting to interrupt.

"And this is Rainy!" Ryder looks toward me and motions me forward. They both stare at me expectantly as I step closer.

"Uh, hi. Nice to meet you." I hold my hand out, unsure how else to interact. Richard scans me with his eyes, as if searching for something more telling. No one moves as I stand there holding out my hand, and it feels like the most dreadful, longest few seconds of my life.

This is embarrassing...

"You must be Ryder's new girlfriend then." He finally takes my hand and firmly shakes it once. His hand is covered with black grease and leaves residue on my own. I have to stop myself from wiping it off on my leg.

My eyes widen as I register his words and I can feel my cheeks suddenly red with heat.

"No, no. She's just a new friend of mine." Ryder laughs.

"Really?" Richard looks at him with a sarcastic tone. "I just assumed because you've never brought someone here before. My mistake."

Richard glances back to me and then to Ryder, studying the both of us. "Richard, Ryder, and Rainy. The three R's. This should be interesting."

Ryder gasps. "I didn't even think of that! This will be great. We'll be like the three musketeers. Or should I say, the three *r*usketeers." He looks to me with a big smile.

Richard shakes his head, not even trying to hide the obvious annoyance on his face. But he seems to tolerate him.

"Well come along. I'll give you a tour of the place." Richard turns around as we follow behind him.

***

Richard is an older man with a stern demeanor and a gray beard to show for it. I don't quite understand their relationship. Ryder is the complete opposite of Richard, yet Ryder seems to enjoy everything about him and even seems happier and more at ease just being around him. I don't really get it because Richard has been nothing but cold since we got here.

He shows us the inside of his house. It's cluttered and disorganized with old furniture, newspapers, and dusty books, which leads me to believe that he definitely lives alone.

The man is a hoarder.

He shows me to a small bathroom and says that we're welcome to it and the shower for as long as we're here— as long as we don't use up all of the hot water, that is. He then takes us to the barn beside the house which is even more cluttered with different tools and old rusted cars. I look around, trying to decipher exactly what kind of work we'll be doing here. Nothing has been revealed of that yet (unless we're expected to clean up his messy house.)

"Ryder, why don't you take her to the greenhouse and show her around while I finish up my work here," Richard suggests as he lifts up a hood to one of the rusted cars.

"Sounds good. We'll meet you back here for grub?"

Richard nods without looking up, already invested in his work.

Ryder leads me to the large greenhouse that occupies most of the space. He lifts up the plastic cover for me to get inside, and as soon as I step in, I'm met with even more confusion. Hot humid air hits my face as I take it all in. Large plants are lined in rows along the ground with big white fans blowing on all four corners of the tent. I finally realize what the plants are when the smell of skunk combined and sweet tones of citrus meet my nose.

"So, this is a weed farm?" I finally ask as I observe the leaves of one of them.

"Yeah... I would have told you but I wasn't sure how you would react," he says sheepishly.

I narrow my eyes at him. "It's definitely not what I expected. What kind of work are we doing here then?"

"My job is usually to take care and maintain the plants. I was thinking you could trim the bud."

"And what does that mean?"

"After harvesting, you would trim off the excess leaves before and after drying," he explains.

I study each plant and try to wrap my head around it. "Won't we get in trouble for something like this?" I seem to have very limited knowledge on marijuana because my mind is coming up completely blank.

Ryder laughs and shakes his head. "Weed has been legal out here for a while now. This entire operation is completely legal, I promise you."

I let out a breath of relief.

"Don't worry. It's a good paying job and I can already tell Richard likes you."

I snort. "Yeah, right. I don't think that man likes anybody."

Ryder laughs again, for much longer now. "Trust me. Once you get to know him, you'll start to understand how he is. He may look like a grump on the outside, but he's just a gentle teddy bear on the inside."

I giggle at the thought and the image of Richard dressed in a giant teddy bear costume comes to mind. It does make me feel a bit better about him.

"Now come on. Let's head back. I have a feeling that Richard is gonna make his famous chili tonight."

I follow Ryder outside, relief washing out me as I step out of the hot muggy tent. It almost makes the desert heat feel bearable.

"So, what do you think? Not too shabby for an odd job huh?" He asks as we walk back toward the barn.

I shrug, still uncertain on how I feel about it. I don't have much of an opinion on weed. None that I can remember anyway. "I guess we'll just have to see how it goes."

Ryder nudges me playfully, making me grab his arm for balance. "That's the spirit!" He winks.

And for just this moment, it feels like everything will be okay.

CHAPTER 19

Rainy

Time doesn't exist within this prison. No matter how hard I try, I can never keep track of how much of it has passed. There is nothing to gauge whether it's been months, weeks, or days. Coya was always the one who would somehow know when we would be fed, when we needed to be quiet, and when the orange suits would return. She would always warn us beforehand and somehow, she was always right.

Now we're left completely in the dark; in both the literal and metaphorical sense, and it's just another dreadful reminder that she's gone.

I can't tell how long it's been since she was taken. We've been fed a couple of times since. How they can sustain us on so little food is another mystery in itself.

Ryder's theory is that they give us some kind of super food and water, packed with everything we need to keep us alive without it for a long time. That would explain the weird flavor and textures.

Each time they brought us food, I took the opportunity and used all my strength to interrogate the orange suits. I screamed into their shielded faces and even spat at them, watching it splatter all over their plastic face cover. Yet, they didn't react, not one word or even a flinch.

I half expected them to reattach the tube to my back, but they never did. The lack of response was infuriating. What happened to all of the cruel intimidation? To all the harsh punishment? There's been nothing. No sign of Cock-eye, no sign of answers.

Just a long, silent waiting game.

The silence is almost physically painful, almost worse than any other torment they have inflicted on us. Knowing that Coya is gone and that anything could be happening to her and there's nothing I can do about it has made me feel utterly hopeless. The confidence and certainty I had felt about our escape before has seemed to disappear along with her.

Ryder has tried to uplift my spirits with more of his stories of the outside world and encouraging words about how we'll escape. But even his optimism has seemed to dwindle as the silence has dragged on. Or perhaps he was being brave for my sake all along? I'm not sure.

I bang my head against the cold concrete wall. Counting each thud as I do it over and over again to distract myself.

I feel disgusting. *I am disgusting.*

The smell of mine and Ryder's waste is impossible to escape. You would think that after being down here so long, I would eventually become nose-blind to it. But unfortunately, that hasn't been the case. And since we haven't been taken out of the room since our last encounter with Cock-eye, the mess hasn't been cleaned up in only god knows how long.

Bang, Bang.

I continue banging the back of my head into the wall. The sound of its thud and the mild pain it brings is the only thing drowning out the silence.

I can't stand feeling my knotted, disgusting hair press against the back of my damp neck any longer. It takes everything in me not to rip it out. *I'm disgusting.*

Bang, Bang.

When will this end?

Bang, Bang.

"Rainy, please. You have to stop. You're gonna hurt yourself." Ryder's soft pleading voice fills the void.

Bang, Bang.

I can hear his words but my mind doesn't seem to want to process or respond to them. My head lifts to bang against the wall again, but the now sudden sweet sound of buttons beeping stops me.

Are they bringing us food again? Are we being taken to Cock-eye? Are they finally bringing Coya back to us? My thoughts race with all of the possibilities as I watch the lights flicker on and the door swing open.

I'd be happy with anything at this point. Even being taken to Cock-eye would be better than this soul-sucking silence.

A sea of orange floods the room with loud urgency as their feet marches forward. My heart leaps into my throat as two large groups open both of our cells. I quickly stand up, wanting to cooperate to the best of my ability. Anything to get me out of this room, away from the stench, *and away from the silence.*

They drag us out of our cells and stand us side by side before commanding us to walk ahead. We do as they command and begin walking forward as the orange suits make a big circle surrounding us. We walk up the steps and outside of the room. For the first time I can see more than just the shiny white tile floor at my feet. The lack of not having a bag over my head brings me a small prick of fear for the unknown. I have to admit that I have grown a sense of familiarity with our small routine, bag over the head and taken to the Light room. But this time is different.

It's hard to focus on my fear as we exit a hallway and enter a massive room with many, many floors. My eyes move through the large facility in front of us. If I hadn't known any better, I would think we were in a Skyscraper. *A Skyscraper underground, if that were possible.* The main floor we are standing on is crowded with different large machines that look like they are meant for flight, and unrecognizable technology. Above us the hundreds of floors appear as though they seemingly lead to nowhere.

"Where are you taking us?" Ryder's voice yells over the stomping of many feet.

"Quiet!" One of the orange suits snarls back at him.

I can feel Ryder tense up as we walk shoulder to shoulder. His eyes are frantically searching the large facility, as though he's looking for something, or *someone*.

"Time is of the essence and we cannot afford to waste it any longer." Cock-eye appears in front of us, seemingly out of thin air with two more orange suits by his side. His chilling voice brings shivers down my spine.

I truly hate this man.

Ryder tries to lunge at him, but the circle of orange suits blocks his way. "Where are you taking us, you fucker?!" he yells through gritted teeth.

Cock-eye lets out a sound that almost resembles a laugh but is not quite right.

"Tn, tn, tn." He clicks his tongue with disapproval. "Ryder, when will you learn not to defy me? It really is a shame. But not to worry. We will take care of your disobedience soon enough." He strides closer to us, his pale gray skin peeling back into an unnaturally wide smile as his lanky body hunches over to peer down at us. It almost makes his eyes look semi-normal as each dark pupil stares downward.

"We have created a much more secure enclosure for the two of you, which will allow us to finally begin the long-awaited harvesting process." He continues in a prideful dark tone. "Some important people have patiently waited for this, and we cannot afford to make them wait any longer."

My stomach drops. Harvesting process? The words make me sick to my stomach as I try to imagine what they could possibly mean.

"I would suggest that you say your goodbyes to each other now. I'm afraid that you will not see each other again after today." Cock-eye's voice finishes smugly.

The world around me freezes. *No. This can't be happening.*

My ears begin ringing as my body suddenly moves without any hesitation alongside Ryder as we try to fight and break out of the barrier of orange bodies blocking us.

"No!" I feel myself scream without realizing. They can't separate us. They just can't. The possibility is more frightening than even death.

Ryder somehow manages to knock down an orange suit and grabs my hand to force our way out of the crowd. "Contain them!" I can hear Cock-eye yell but it's muffled by the sound of our running feet and the loud ringing in my ears.

"We need to find a way out of here!" Ryder shouts as we continue running. We dodge past the different large machines and run into a winding tunnel with brown stone walls that fork into many different paths. Taking the farthest path, we run until we can't hear them chasing behind us.

All those days trapped in that dark room; I wished I could run more than anything. This isn't quite what I had in mind, running for my life.

I'm breathing heavily and my blood is racing hard through my veins, so hard that it's difficult to think.

As we make our way through the tunnel, I can hear a loud constant swishing sound in the distance that suddenly calms the ringing in my ears for only a brief moment.

It sounds like running water...

Without saying a word, we both walk toward it. The sound getting louder and louder with each step we take. We turn left and are suddenly met face-to-face with a massive waterfall tucked against the rocky wall.

The waterfall descends from far above and crashes into the ground violently, disappearing as it falls.

"It's so beautiful..." My whisper can barely be heard over its rhythmic crashing. Who would have ever thought that something like this could exist in this horrible place. *What is it even doing here?*

We're at a dead-end and there's nowhere else to go. I step closer to the waterfall, a light mist of water droplets sprinkles onto my face, sending bursts of energy throughout my entire body. All I want to do is dip my head in and drink until my heart's content. But I can't focus on that now.

"What do we do now?" I manage to say through labored breaths. My body aches all over and if it weren't for the adrenaline coursing through me, I'm sure I would collapse.

"Rainy, look at me." Ryder cups my cheeks with both hands and forces my eyes on him. His body is trembling and his palms are slick with sweat. "You need to warp us out of here. You need to think about any of the places I described to you and take us there."

The ringing in my ears returns and is intensified with the thought of escaping. I shake my head as tears pool into my eyes. I can suddenly hear the running footsteps drawing closer to us. "Don't let them near it!" Cock-eyes inhuman voice booms from a distance.

"No, we can't leave Coya behind! We have to find her!" I sob. "We promised we would all escape together."

Ryder keeps my eyes on his and for a moment, I don't recognize him. "That doesn't matter now. We don't have time. We're going to die if we stay here." He urges me. "Think of a place, Rainy."

His words break my heart as they start to register. How could he betray her again? How could he betray our promise? *There has to be another way.*

I open my mouth to convince him otherwise but we're suddenly surrounded by orange suits once again. They immediately grab us and try to pull us apart.

I hold on to Ryder's hands for dear life, afraid to let go.

"Rainy, please!" Ryder yells through the chaos.

I close my eyes and try to imagine any of the places he described to me, as quickly as possible. The loud ringing screams inside my ears and a familiar pressure builds against my skull as images of places flood my mind. Cities, forestry mountains, *a barren desert...*

My eyes fly open when I feel Ryder's hands losing grip. His eyes fill with fear. "No!" He screams, and for a moment I think it's because we're being separated, but then suddenly a cold sharp object jabs into my temple. A zapping sound is all I hear before everything turns black.

***

Where am I? I don't exactly remember waking up. I don't exactly remember anything. I sit up and cough for some time, gasping for air. Beads of sweat drip down my face and onto the ground. It's so dry. It's so hot and my body aches all over.

I look around and there's nothing. Just dirt and more dirt, some plants and rocks, and— oh look a rabbit!

The gray rabbit freezes as it watches me attempt to stand before it hops away. Sharp pains and weakness spread throughout my body, causing me to sway as I slowly struggle to my feet. It takes everything in me to try and keep balance.

The rabbit seems to disappear among the brush. I don't follow it. Instead, I decide it's better if I try to find food and water. Anything to make these uncomfortable feelings and pains go away.

I glance down and study my hands and clothes. My hands look bizarre and unfamiliar. My body and clothes are caked with dirt and muck, making the uncomfortable feelings double. I try not to dwell on it too long.

The Forgetful Rain

I need food and water... I feel so weak...

CHAPTER 20

Maze

We're sitting next to a fire as Richard serves us bowls of chili, he spent the last few hours preparing for us.

"Thank you so much. It smells delicious." I try to make small talk as he hands me a bowl. He nods his head without responding and settles in across from us.

The fire illuminates our faces in the dark as we eat. I blow on my spoon and take a bite. The spicy, savory flavor is like nothing I've ever had before and I involuntarily make sounds of approval.

"Oh my god," I catch myself saying.

"I told you. Richard makes the best chili in the world," Ryder manages to say between bites. "Nothing beats it."

Richard rolls his eyes and focuses on me. "It's simple and the only thing I know how to make a lot of. So don't expect much else." His voice is cold but I try not to take it personally, remembering what Ryder said earlier. *I don't understand how a man like him can make something that tastes this good.*

I can't help but scarf my food down while awkwardly keeping my eyes on the fire and away from Richard's sharp, piercing stare.

"So where is it you're from?" His flat voice breaks the silence. I look back up at him, startled by his question and unsure how to answer.

"She's a traveler like me. With no real destination and no real home to return to," Ryder answers before I get a chance to, and I'm thankful for it.

"I see..." Richard looks between the both of us, with eyes that say he's not really buying it. "So then Rainy, do you smoke?" His words remind me of the man from the truck who offered me a cigarette the first day I woke up. I shake my head.

"Good. Don't need anybody smoking up the merchandise," he says as he pulls out a glass pipe and lighter from his pocket and proceeds to smoke what's inside of it.

Ryder turns to face me. "Richard prefers to have people who don't smoke work for him. So that works out great for us." He gives me a reassuring smile.

I force a smile back then turn my attention to Richard. He blows out a thick cloud of smoke in our direction. I try not to breathe it in as it reaches my face and I resist the urge to wave it away. Something tells me that he might find that disrespectful in some way.

I'm somewhat relieved. Part of me wondered if I would be expected to smoke the different types of weed here after learning about the work we would be doing. I wasn't prepared to explore what that might do to my already fragile memory.

"So, where is it ya'll met?" Richard coughs out.

"We met at a cafe," I say, surprising myself by how quickly I answered. "How did you guys meet?" I repeat the question to him, hoping to divert the conversation from me.

Ryder laughs. "Now that's a good story." He spoons more chili into his mouth and looks to Richard to tell it. I stare at Richard expectantly as he fumbles with the glass pipe in his hand.

"I almost hit him with my truck," he states nonchalantly after a few moments, picking off small pieces of weed from his tongue.

My eyes widen in response and I'm suddenly intrigued to hear the rest of the story.

Ryder bursts out with more laughter. "Man, why do you always say it like that? It wasn't that big of a deal."

Richard shrugs, looking much more relaxed now.

"So then, what happened?" I ask.

"It happened a couple years ago. I was driving back home one night and this dumbass walked right out in front of me in the middle of nowhere." He glances at him, his blue eyes more intense than before. "He's lucky I didn't hit him. When I pulled over, he didn't know where he was or what was happenin. So, I took him in until he could figure his shit out."

Ryder stretches his arms, amused by the story. "Yup! And he hasn't been able to get rid of me since."

"How did you get out there in the first place?" I ask. Shock runs through me as I realize the similarity.

He shrugs. "Partied too hard and wandered off, I guess. But anyway, I'm happy you were the one who found me; otherwise, I would have never gotten to taste this amazing chili." He spoons what's left in his bowl into his mouth.

Richard stands up and grabs the empty bowls from us. "Yeah well, sometimes I wish I really did hit ya," he grumbles, but Ryder just laughs it off. "I'm retiring for the night. I expect I'll see y'all in the morning bright and early," he says as he walks off.

"Yup. See ya in the morning!" Ryder calls back.

The thought of waking up early again exhausts me, but I say nothing in protest. Ryder puts out the fire with a hose and we walk back to the van in silence. Part of me wants to ask him more about how they met. I can tell he's not giving up the whole story, making me wonder if there's some resemblance to my situation. Then again, I also don't want to give him the impression that I don't trust him.

We get inside the van and are soon sitting side by side on the bed.

"So, what do you think?"

"Of what?" I ask, my mind too scrambled to pinpoint what he's referring to.

He cocks his head to the side, a small hint of a smirk pulling on his lips. "Of this place! What do you think of the job and Richard?"

I can't tell if he's searching for some sort of approval from me. We've been here for only a few hours so I'm still just trying to figure it all out. As far as I'm aware, I don't have any prior experience or anything to compare or relate any of this to. But I'm trying not to let it overwhelm me.

"I don't know. It seems fine. Does Richard live out here all alone?" I say, trying to change the subject.

"Yup, that's how he likes it. He never married or anything. He's more of a loner and doesn't like being around people much."

"He seems to like you though," I say, thinking back to earlier when Richard had let his guard down for a glimpse of a moment after Ryder hugged him.

Ryder smiles fondly, his single dimple deepening. "Yeah, well, what's not to like?" he jokes and I roll my eyes.

"And that was nice of him to take you in when you had first met," I add after a few moments, hoping to get more out of him.

He nods, saying nothing as he unties his black boots.

"Why is it that you guys get along so well? He seems like an impossible man to please."

Ryder shrugs. "I don't really know. We just do. Plus, we've gotten pretty close throughout the years. Once I had to take care of him for a couple of months when he got really sick." He suddenly frowns at the thought, making my heart sink. I really don't like seeing him upset.

"What happened?"

He shakes his head as if to physically shake away the memory. "He had a form of cancer that really messed him up for a while. But he's all better now." He forces a small smile to reassure me.

"That's good. I'm happy you both found each other." I smile back.

"But anyway, we won't be here for long. Once we save enough money, we'll be back on the road in no time!" He stretches out, letting his body fall on the bed as he closes his eyes and rests his hands underneath his head.

I peer down at him. His brown hair reaches past his chin and has a slight shine from not being washed. I can't help myself from noticing his soft features and unblemished skin. You would never know that he spends most of his time outside in the sun if it weren't for the creamy brown color of his tan. Without realizing, my eyes rest on his full lips and I catch myself almost imagining what they might feel like against mine.

"Are you excited to go to Alaska?" he asks, opening his eyes again.

I nod, peeling my gaze away. "Yeah, it's all I can think about." *Among other things.*

"Me too. I don't think I've ever been this excited for a trip."

I arch an eyebrow. "Really?" My heart jumps knowing that that must be saying a lot considering how many trips he's been on. *Could it be because I'm going with?*

"Of course. I've heard stories about Alaska and how beautiful it is. I've always wanted to go."

"Oh..." I don't know why I expected a different answer. I don't know why I let myself think that his excitement might have been caused by me being there. I try to hide my disappointment as I lay beside him, leaving space between us.

Ryder turns off his portable lamp and settles in. The van is completely dark except for the subtle glow seeping in through the windows. It's quieter here than it was where we were the night before. The crickets aren't chirping as loud and my heart isn't pounding as hard.

I lay very still on my back, allowing my mind to wander. I wait patiently, half expecting Ryder to turn toward me and hold me like the night before. But he doesn't.

"Goodnight, Ryder," I whisper.

"Goodnight," he mumbles.

I turn away from him and toward the wall, gripping the blanket close to my face. It was silly of me to have thought he might have wanted to hold me again. Maybe he didn't like that I was lying on top of him when we woke up this morning.

Or maybe he has decided he doesn't like me in that way after all...

***

The next morning is cooler than the one before. The farm looks brighter and more cheerful against the early sun and to my surprise, waking up wasn't as difficult as I expected either.

I sip warm coffee from a little mug that Ryder woke me up with as we're waiting outside the greenhouse for Richard. The bittersweet liquid warms my chest as it makes its way down my throat, bringing me a euphoric comfort. I clasp the mug with both hands and hold it to my nose, breathing in the sweet scent mixed with the crisp morning air.

Richard meets us at the entrance before we make our way inside to start our work. They both show me how to trim the bud and where to lay it out to dry, all of the ins and outs of what's expected of me before leaving me to it.

Ryder stations himself on the other side of the tent as he tends to the plants. I stare down at the bucket in front of me, pruning shears in one hand, small branch of weed in the other. My fingers are already coated in stickiness as I begin my work.

Trimming is more relaxing and therapeutic than I would have thought. It gives me time to think while simultaneously being able to not think at all.

My only complaint would be that it's almost impossible to be able to talk to Ryder through the buzzing of loud fans and the distance between us across the tent. He doesn't seem to mind much though, his face is focused, zoned in on the plant he's watering. I divert my gaze back to my hands and force myself to stay glued to my work, occasionally glancing back over until I finally meet his eyes. He gives me a small smile and a wink before returning his attention to the plant.

That's all of the reassurance I need. An ache gnaws at my heart as I hold my breath and continue my trimming.

CHAPTER 21

Ryder

She just vanished. One moment her hands were gripping mine then the next, she was just gone. As if she had never existed here in the first place. When she had warped into her cell before, I was amazed by it. I wasn't looking directly at her when she manifested out of thin air, so I couldn't really take it in or see it happen. It was hard to believe, I almost didn't believe her for a while. But there was no other explanation for how she got there. And for the first time since I escaped, it gave me hope.

But this time was different. Seeing her disappear right in front of me was both unbelievable and heartbreaking.

"Where is she, *Ryder*?" Cock-eyes slimy voice muffles in and out in front of me, coated with anger. But truly, I couldn't care less.

She's gone, and I'm stuck here.

Cock-eye isn't his real name. I can't remember what his real name is or when we started calling him that, just that it had made me laugh anytime Coya or I would say it. Somehow it lessened the terrors the thought of him brought. Knowing he was at the mercy of a stupid (yet fitting) joke gave us the smallest bit of joy. It's all you can really do in this place, find the smallest bits of joy hidden within the cracks of torture. *If you can.*

Maybe if it were years ago and I was still afraid of him, I would have immediately listened and followed his orders. I was a weak kid back then and all I ever knew was fear, because of him. But after I escaped and learned that there's more out there than just pain and fear, his voice lost almost all of its power over me. *Almost.* The rest was lost when I saw him almost hurt *her*. Something came over me, something that wouldn't allow me to let that happen.

"Ryder... Don't you want to see her again?" This time his voice catches my attention. I can already tell where this is going. He's gonna try to bribe me and use her against me. I know how his mind works and his little games and tricks. After seeing me protect her from him, he saw it as a weakness and boy, does he love taking advantage of my weaknesses. *I just hope that I'm strong enough not to let him get to me...*

I glance up at his twisted face standing over me. Orange suits crowd around us, ready to jump in if I make any sudden movements. I'm seated on the ground, my arms tied behind my back, giving me very little mobility. If I wanted to try anything, I probably couldn't.

At this point, I just feel defeated. I really thought we had a chance at escaping *together*. It was just a hunch, but I thought if I described to her some of the places I had been and was touching her as she warped— I don't know... I just thought we could both disappear from here. It made sense at the time. She had said that she could only appear back in her cell because it was the only other place she knew of. And I guess it partially worked because she isn't anywhere near here anymore. I can't *feel* her here anymore...

She left me.

"Did you hear me? Speak, *parasite*. " Cock-eye growls, waiting for a response from me.

"You were going to separate us," I spit back. It's all I can think of to say. It's the only anger I can allow myself to hone in on.

He makes a nightmarish smirk, pondering on my words for a moment. "What if we can make a deal? I know you can sense where she is..."

My eyes glare into him as my heart thumps hard in my chest. He's right, but how did he know?

I could feel her and almost navigate where she was. I don't know how, but it's as if a part of her lingers somewhere inside me, and the rest of her is somewhere else. It's as if I can see through her eyes and feel what she's feeling. I could feel it the moment she disappeared but I wasn't sure what it was until now.

"What do you want?" A low whisper escapes my throat, betraying me.

His inhuman smile spreads wider across his ugly face, making me want to gag. But the anticipation for what he's about to say next overpowers my disgust.

"We'll let you go and we'll let you find her."

My eyes widen. *He can't be serious.*

"But..." He lingers, toying with me. "You have to bring her back to me." And there it is. The sick twisted game he wants to play to get what he wants. It's not gonna happen.

"Fuck you! Why the hell would I do that? I'm not doing shit for you." Anger boils in me. *He must be even stupider than I thought.*

"Because if you do, I'll let you go for good." He finishes with a smug look on his face.

My mouth goes dry, stopping me abruptly.

The thought of freedom, true freedom without always having to be on the run or having to hide. That was something I've always wanted, something I've always dreamed of. A distant dream that I knew would never come. It was too good to be true.

"You're lying." This is just another part of his tricks. He would never consider letting me go and I have to continue reminding myself of that. No matter how tempting his promises might be. I know better than anybody that his promises come with a price.

"I know it's hard to believe, but truly I've got all that I want from you. You're more trouble to me than you are useful," he explains and waits for me to answer. I say nothing.

"It's either this or death." The cold words slither out of his mouth.

My body freezes. I know what he is saying has to be true. There's not a single hint of deceit within his voice. Cock-eye is many things, but I've never known him to be a liar. Am I prepared to die for her?

She left me.

"Bring her back to me and I will even give you back your precious memories from your time before here, then set you free." He sweetens the deal.

Everything inside me is at war with itself.

Her eyes fill my mind. Her sweet voice. The way she looked at me. The way she said my name. The touch of her skin.

She will never know what she meant to me all those days inside that room, inside that *prison*. How she gave me a reason to wake up, a reason to keep going. She made me feel alive again. She gave me hope.

But then she left me. Abandoned me. Left me here. *Alone.*

What the fuck do I do?

I imagine the feeling of sun against my skin, earth beneath my feet. The feeling of being on the road, and sleeping beneath the stars. Running with the wind in my hair, and swimming in an endless ocean. I remember the sweet sound of music, and the magical touch of *rain.* Being able to see farther than just a few feet in front of me, and more than just the cold soul-sucking concrete. Being able to finally explore a wide and mysterious Earth...There's so much more for me to see, so much more for me to explore and experience. I haven't even begun to scratch the surface of it all.

Forgive me.

I meet his eyes, searching for the slightest bit of betrayal within them. He holds my gaze, a wide knowing grin unfaltering on his face.

"Tick, tick, tick. Time is running out." He taps his wrist. His eyes bulge out of his head, showing the white around his crooked pupil. It makes him look like a starving junky, desperate for his dope.

I breathe slowly. I can feel her inside me, pulling me to her. Somehow, I know exactly where she is and how to find her. She's not too far, her eyes have just opened revealing everything around her and I can see images of desert flash through my mind.

This isn't gonna be easy but I have no other choice. *It's this or death...*

"Fine. You got a deal."

CHAPTER 22

Maze

Today is the first day it's been overcast since I woke up in the middle of the desert over a week ago. The gray clouds hang thick and heavy, leaving no remnants of a once-blue sky. I lean back in the lawn chair, breathing in the moist air. I have to admit that the possibility of rain makes me almost giddy.

It's also the first day I've had off from trimming weed since we started working here. The week went by so fast. Working nonstop melded the days together like putty and for the first time, I finally have some time to myself.

Ryder has been gone for most of the day grocery shopping for Richard. Richard explained that he takes a trip to buy food and supplies at least once a week. Today, Ryder volunteered to go for him instead. Since he's left,

Richard has spent the day by himself. Not that I'm complaining. I don't usually see much of him anyway, other than in the greenhouse or in passing when I'm using his bathroom. And when I do, he never has much to say to me.

I pick up my can of coke from off the ground and take a big gulp from it. I watch the clouds drift slowly by, vivid and full of life, while they seem to take deep breaths across the sky. The usual harsh sun is hiding today, allowing me to sit out in the open desert field near the farm, where I can watch the sky and feel at peace.

Outside of working, I haven't found much time to talk or spend with Ryder. We've both been so busy during the day and then exhausted by night that we usually fall right to sleep by the time we're back in the van. I'm really starting to miss the brief moments we spent alone together by the lake. *I'm missing him...* Yet, he seems to go on unbothered. He's been different somehow since we got here. Distant in some ways. I'd like to think that it's just because of all the work we've been doing...but something tells me it's more than that.

A bolt of lightning flashes across the sky above me, with it a loud cracking boom of thunder. I finish my coke and decide it's probably best to go inside.

I walk toward the house hoping to find another soda in the fridge when I get inside. On the way there, my eyes catch Richard sitting in the small garage on the right side of the house.

He doesn't seem to notice me and proceeds to dip his fingers into a small container of paint before slowly spreading them across a canvas with ease.

I walk up quietly, drawn to the sight. I watch him as he takes his time with each stroke and without any hesitation, alternating between fingers and paint brush.

Once I'm right behind him I can see the painting clearly, bursting with vibrant colors and textured lines. It's abstract and colorful, an unexpected surprise to what I would have imagined Richard would paint— given that seeing him painting in the first place is a surprise in itself.

"Looks beautiful." The words escape my mouth. He turns to face me, unfazed by my sudden interruption. Blotches of dry paint stain his leathery skin, creasing with his wrinkles as his brows furrow.

"It's not no Picasso, but it's something," he says, turning back to look at it as if viewing it for the very first time.

"Do you paint?" he asks, using a pinpoint paintbrush to touch up small details.

"No," I answer to the best of my knowledge.

He gets up and walks over to the other side of the garage, grabbing another canvas and more paint. He replaces his painting with the blank canvas on the stand, then steps back and motions me over to the seat.

I shake my head. "Oh no, that's alright. I don't wanna waste your supplies."

He huffs and stares me down. "When someone offers you something, accepting it is usually the polite thing to do. Besides, this oughta give you something else to do besides sittin' around doing nothin'."

I give in and sit down, not wanting to be scolded by him any longer. I eye the small blank canvas in front of me. "What am I supposed to paint?"

"Whatever you want. You can paint anything and everything. That's the beauty of it." He pauses. "Just not no damn stick figures."

I smile slightly, holding in a laugh. "Okay. Thank you."

He nods, then turns and walks toward the house, leaving me alone with the canvas and paint, unsure what to do with myself. *Well, this day just took a very unexpected turn...*

I stare back at the canvas and container of paint for a few moments, not knowing where to start. Sometime drags on and finally without thinking, I dip the paintbrush in black and spread it everywhere, covering every inch of white. As my hand moves around the canvas, I notice that each movement I make comes fluidly. Each step feels simple and automatic. I hardly notice the constant lightning flashes that burst from behind me, illuminating the small garage with quick flickers of light. I'm completely sucked into what I'm doing, unaware of anything else.

I allow my hands to do as they please, as if they have a mind of their own and have done this time and time again. They glide across the canvas, with each stroke more confident than the last.

As I paint, I realize that this is the first thing I've done that has felt normal and almost nostalgic since I woke up in the desert with no memory. It seems to come to me as naturally as breathing and eating. It's as if I was always meant to do this, and the paintbrush is just an extension of my arm, moving with very little instruction.

I'm not sure how much time has passed or how long I have been painting for. I lean against the chair and rest my neck, doing well not touching anything with my stained fingers.

Who would have thought that something as simple as painting would feel so exhilarating? So normal?

Is this what it feels like to be certain of yourself?

"Wow, Rainy. I didn't know you could paint like that." Ryder's voice startles me and I turn to see him standing behind me with Richard a few feet away. *I guess this is karma for having snuck up on Richard before.*

"Your girl sure does have some talent," Richard says, his eyes on the painting and his expression unreadable.

I swallow, feeling my cheeks quickly blush in response. Ryder leans in over me to examine the painting closer. He's close enough that I can feel the warmth emanating from his skin, sending the increasing heat in my cheeks spiraling.

"How long have you guys been standing there?" I say, my voice almost failing me.

"I just got here but it looked like Richard had been here for a while."

"I came in to grab something and decided to stick around to see the finished product," Richard replies dryly.

"Well, it looks like you definitely have some competition on your hands, old man." Ryder straightens himself, laughing as he steps back.

Richard shrugs lazily, unamused. "I'm just happy to see *someone* around here has some potential."

Ryder scoffs, pretending that he's been struck in the heart. "Awe, come on. Don't be like that! I have potential! You just haven't seen my stellar dance moves yet," he jokes dramatically, waving his arms around while tapping his foot with no rhythm.

Richard shakes his head, his guard almost dropping once again. A small hint of a smile tugs at his lips, but he quickly turns away. "You're a dumbass," he grumbles before leaving the garage.

"He's just jealous." Ryder laughs, turning back to me.

I can't hold it in any longer and without warning, I burst out laughing uncontrollably. Seeing Ryder attempt to dance and watching Richard almost break from his hard exterior. Combined with my embarrassment of being watched and praised for my painting. I guess it all bottled up inside of me and I exploded. I laugh so hard that my sides begin to hurt and it takes everything in me to finally calm down.

Ryder's eyes burn into me, a big smirk plastered on his face.

"Sorry, that was just so funny," I manage to say while wiping tears from the corners of my eyes.

"Don't apologize, I love your laugh. I think that's the first time I've actually ever heard it." He stares at me, unmoving.

I look away, feeling the embarrassment take over once again. *Maybe he does feel something for me...*

"Come on. Let's let your painting dry and wash up for grub," he says as he walks out. I stand up to follow him but stop to glance at the painting one last time.

It portrays a hyperrealistic night. The black sky almost swallows everything up inside of it except for the scattered stars and hazy lights that huddle together along the bottom. It's the exact same view from Ryder's favorite lookout.

I almost can't believe that I'm the one who painted it. I had allowed my physical body to take over while seemingly existing on autopilot. My mind was mostly present, but another part of me felt like it was somewhere else, existing on a completely different plane. I try not to dwell on it as I follow Ryder outside.

We make our way toward the house, but before we can reach the front door, rain begins pouring down like an unrelenting monsoon. Without warning, we're quickly swallowed whole by the enticing smell of wet earth that is finally relieved of its thirst and drought.

We're immediately surrounded by the screaming sound of raindrops smacking into the ground, drowning everything else around us. Ryder looks at me as the biggest smile spreads across his face.

"Not quite what I had in mind to wash up but this will work!" he shouts loud enough for me to hear. He grabs my hand and pulls me toward the open desert, the raindrops coating us in seconds.

"Let loose in the rain, Rainy!" he yells, laughing.

Without hesitation, I instantly comply. We start running, jumping and skipping around— dancing with the rain like small children. Something about the way the rain feels against my skin brings me an indescribable rush of energy, as if I have just drunk two cups of coffee right before cliff jumping.

I'm overcome with joy that it's finally raining, but also that I'm finally seeing the side of Ryder that I've missed so much, the side I had met back at the lake and worried might have disappeared along with it.

I watch him let go of my hand and dance around happily with his arms in the air, his hair and clothes soaked and clinging to his body.

"Is that those *stellar moves* you were talking about?" I yell, giggling.

He stops abruptly and stands still for a moment, staring into me with a look in his eyes I don't recognize.

Did I say something wrong?

He steps closer until he's right in front of me and takes my face with both hands. I'm frozen by his gentle touch. He stands over me and lingers for a moment, water dripping from his wet hair and onto my face. Then before I can get a word out or even think, he leans down and kisses me.

CHAPTER 23

15 years ago
Ryder

The man is so scary. He comes in and out of the room over and over, just staring at me before leaving again. He has a scary face and he's the only one of them that doesn't wear a rubber suit.

I don't know how I got here or when, just that I'm always hungry and scared, and *I hate it here.*

I'm strapped down to a hard bed, my legs tied down and my arms restrained to my sides. I've been laying like this for a long time, long enough for my whole underside to go numb and tingle whenever I try to move.

For a long time, I'm alone like this until the door flies open and the scary man walks in with the others wearing suits covering their bodies and faces. This time the man doesn't look at me and instead talks to the others while touring the room. It's as if I'm not even there as he gestures around formally.

"As you can see, we have settled quite nicely on this base." The scary man speaks to the suited bodies surrounding him as they move throughout the large room. "We have been making progress here even faster than we have with other habitable planets in the past. The Hominin here are especially docile and governable. We have already introduced them to greater forms of technology and media, which in only the last century or two, they have grown with exponentially. Keeping themselves happily ignorant while we've taken leadership, just as we hoped."

The man continues speaking but it's hard to pay attention to anything he's saying. I try to breathe quietly so that I won't bring any attention to myself. I wish I could move, my whole body aches from laying still too long.

"We have also introduced them to much more powerful weaponry, enough so to keep them at war with themselves, harming each other and their wretched planet in the process. They have continued to poison their own food, water, and air, all while keeping themselves distracted by their growing technology, wealth, and petty politics. This allows us to stay in power to continue our task. So far, it's been a very successful process and as you can see, while constructing a base at this location, by luck, a vessel arrived close enough that we were able to detect and though, unfortunately, we were only able to retrieve this *rider* —" The group stops in front of me as he motions a hand over my entire body.

"He is the first full-blooded Nixie we have been able to obtain in centuries." The man concludes proudly. The group behind him gasps and I can barely make out their dark shielded eyes as they widen with surprise.

The man lifts a hand to silence them while staring intently at me with one eye as the other stares permanently toward the ground. "He may only be a small juvenile for now, but he will grow, and while we wait for his growth, we will continue to search for others. Our Searchers have detected many Nixie descendants on this planet, as well as vessels continuing to come and go. We will obtain more with time." His voice drops low with promise, his eye never leaving mine.

"Sir?" One of the suited bodies speaks up, dragging the man's attention away from me. He turns his head slowly around toward their direction.

"Yesss?" The word slithers out of his mouth, making me wish more than anything that I could disappear.

"Will we be given Hominin faces as well?"

A wide scary smile pulls on the man's face, spreading from one ear to the next. "Ah, yes. If you do well of course. The Hominins here may be imbeciles but they are no longer primitive. You must do well to hide our existence and most importantly, our purpose." The man begins to walk to the other side of me, directing them to follow behind.

"You must be careful. Their faces are fragile and very impressionable— for example." They stop walking abruptly as the man's hands reach for his face and his fingers pinch both of his cheeks. He pulls them apart as though his skin were malleable slime. He stretches his face, revealing pinkish gray flesh and gooey darkness beneath. The skin leaves his dark eyes and rows of teeth tucked into the pulsing mush.

I begin screaming. I can't stop. Everything about this place is terrifying, but nothing comes close to this man.

Please, please, please. I don't want to be here anymore.

"Silence the *rider*." The man directs. I can't stop screaming as an orange body walks to my side and pierces something into my skin. I continue screaming long after they leave the room and the lights disappear.

I scream until everything fades away.

CHAPTER 24

Maze

I rub the sticky gunk of stubborn resin between my hands, pinching my fingers together to create a little ball of it before flicking it away. No matter how hard I scrub or wash them, nothing ever really does the trick. But slowly I have grown used to the sour earthy smell that clings to my fingers and hides under my nail-beds. Before, I would try to bite the nails away to get rid of it, but my efforts were always useless.

Luckily, I won't have to worry about scrubbing away sticky residue for a while. After working here for a few weeks, Ryder and I have finally finished cutting down and drying the batch of weed that needed processing. It will be a while until the next plants are ready to be harvested.

I look over to Ryder as he studies the glass jars on the table, filled to the brim with our hard work. He catches me looking at him and gives me a smooth side smile that causes my heart to skip a beat.

After he kissed me that day, he pulled away, apologizing and laughing it off as though it had never happened. It left my heart aching. I yearned for more, but didn't know how to find the words. How could I force my tongue to move and let out sounds that would make him understand?

He hasn't kissed me since then, except for the occasional brief pecks on my cheek or forehead when leaving or greeting me. I now cherish those small kisses, searching for a deeper meaning in them— a deeper affection that says more than just the platonic hellos and goodbyes they appear to say.

Richard bursts in from the kitchen bearing a bottle of champagne in one hand, and the other gripping three-different sized glasses.

"It's not much, but I figured we'd drink in celebration of all your work so far," he says as he sets down the glasses and pops open the bottle.

"Wow, old man. Is that a compliment?" Ryder smirks in his charming way as he grabs a glass.

Richard narrows his eyes at him. "Yes actually, for my dear friend Rainy here."

I can't help but laugh at the sarcastic remark as he pours champagne into my glass. "Why thank you,

Richard," I say sweetly. I take a long sip of the bubbly liquid and it warms my chest as it makes its way down.

Ryder was right about Richard. I have gotten used to his hard exterior and learned how to find the soft inside he tries so hard to hide. Ever since that day when I first caught him painting, Richard seemed to warm up to me. He has since set up a second painting stand in the garage next to his and will have me paint with him whenever we're not working or when we have free time.

Most of the time we paint in silence, except for his occasional remarks or my polite comments. At first it was a little awkward, but I've found myself slowly growing fond of those simple moments together. They've shown me a kinder side of the grumpy, reserved man that is Richard.

"I knew it was only a matter of time before the two of you plotted against me." Ryder shakes his head, grinning ear to ear before downing his entire glass in one gulp.

Richard picks up one of the jars from the table, opening and inspecting it before taking a big whiff.

"It's better than the last batch, huh?" Ryder asks, his face full of pride.

"It's not bad." Richard shrugs as he sets it down. He digs into his pocket and pulls out a wad of cash, counting it out to give to us. "One thousand for each of you."

My eyes widen as he hands me the money. I wasn't sure how much we would be getting paid, but a thousand dollars feels like more than enough. "Wow, thank you," I say, not sure what to do with the money in my hands.

Richard arches an eyebrow. "Why would you thank me? It's what I owe you," he says, his voice flat.

"I mean... Thank you for letting us work for you and giving us a place to stay," I stutter. I may have gotten on his good side, but he still knows how to be all cold and intimidating, turning me into a fidgety nervous wreck. It's gonna take a lot of getting used to.

He shrugs again. "I couldn't have done it by myself. So still, there's no need for thanking."

"Wow, Richard. You are just filled with compliments today," Ryder chimes in.

We continue drinking away the champagne as they bicker back and forth in the non-serious way they always do. Ryder says sarcastic but friendly things that he knows will rub Richard the wrong way, while Richard snaps back with eye rolls and snide responses.

My blood heats up with the unfamiliar feeling of alcohol coursing through my veins. It makes me feel lighter, and all the worries I've had seem like a distant memory now.

Right now, I feel like nothing could go wrong. I quickly begin to appreciate this moment with them even more as I watch them speak. My insecurities seemingly melt away and everything feels just right.

"So, where is it ya'll plan to go after you leave here?" Richard's question distracts my daze. I open my mouth, excited to talk about Alaska and the possibility of seeing the Northern lights.

"You know me, onto the next adventure." Ryder shrugs it off quickly before I'm able to say anything.

I shoot him a questioning look but he doesn't seem to notice. Why wouldn't he tell him of our plans to go to Alaska?

Time seems to slip away and after a while, we finish off the bottle and decide it's late enough to head to bed. I try to thank Richard again for the champagne as I say goodnight but he just waves me away as usual. *Note to self, Richard does not like being thanked.*

I follow Ryder outside and we begin making our way back to the van.

The darkness feels heavier to walk through under the shade of alcohol. I try to take my time putting one foot after the other but can feel my body sway a bit as I try to keep balance.

"Why didn't you tell Richard about Alaska?" I ask once we're far enough away from the house. A fuzzy feeling takes over my insides, making me feel like I could say or ask anything without a care in the world.

"I don't know. I didn't wanna jinx it," he says plainly.

"What do you mean?"

"Like when you tell someone your plans for the future, their energy can sometimes affect it or jinx it into not happening."

I start to giggle, unable to stop myself because everything seems funny to me right now. "You say the weirdest stuff sometimes." I try to look at him, but can only make out his tall silhouette in the dark. And something else.

The unnatural glow coming from his eyes.

I try to step closer to him to get a better look but trip on something and almost fall on my face.

Ryder manages to quickly catch me by my arm and it makes me giggle even more at my clumsiness. He loops his arm through mine to help me walk the rest of the way.

"You have a habit of tripping on your own feet." I can hear the amusement in his voice.

"Well, what do you expect? It's pitch black out here," I argue, his glowing eyes now gone and completely forgotten.

We soon make it back to the van. Ryder turns on the portable lamp once we're inside.

I glance at the bed, but my stomach feels too bubbly and excited to want to sleep. I slide onto it anyway and lean my back against the wall, watching him as he puts his money away.

"How much do you think we'll need to make before our trip?" I ask.

He thinks for a moment. "As much as we can, honestly. We'll need money for gas, food, and even more once we actually get there."

I hand him the money from my pocket. "Here. We might as well keep it all together." I smile as he hesitantly takes it.

"Okay well, I'll keep it safe right here if you ever want it," he says as he stuffs it into a pocket attached to the wall across from me.

I watch him closely, studying his broad chest and tan arms as they move, causing all the nerves in my body to heighten and the familiar ache in my heart to return. I don't bother to look away or hide how closely I'm watching him and what it's doing to me.

He starts getting ready for bed, peeling off his shoes and socks. He takes off his shirt to put on a new one, but before he gets a chance to, I crawl closer to him and set my hand on his arm to stop him.

He gives me a confused look, but I speak before he can say anything. "Can you please kiss me again?"

He relaxes his arm, looking into my eyes with what I hope is yearning for the same thing I am. He raises his other arm and softly caresses my cheek with his fingers. An electric shiver shoots through my skin and causes every goosebump on my body to rise, scream, and beg for more of his touch.

"I want to..." he trails off, his voice low and pleading.

"Then do it," I blurt.

He pauses, unmoving. Before he can decide, and before I can talk myself out of it, I grab the back of his neck and pull his lips to mine, kissing him hard with the hunger that has gnawed at me for weeks.

At first, he's stiff and almost resistant as if he might want to pull away, but soon his body relaxes. He wraps his arms around me, kissing me more deeply and simmering it down into a gentle force.

I lay down, pulling him on top of me. I glide my fingers along his back and release his lips to kiss his neck and shoulder. He shudders slightly at the touch, making a groan that sounds one part pleasurable and one part almost painful. His skin tastes salty and warm against my lips, making me crave more.

He follows suit, putting his mouth to my neck and leaving feathery kisses down my jaw to my collarbone. A weak moan escapes my lips underneath his touch.

I can't believe this is happening. I have known that I wanted to be with him but I didn't know that it would feel like this. Each touch we make is soft yet hungry with anticipation, as though neither of us has ever been touched before, and we have been waiting for this our entire lives.

I press myself tightly against him, craving every part of him. I don't think I've ever wanted anything more—not my forgotten life, memory, nothing.

I want him. I want all of him. *Please let this moment last forever...*

My fingers trail down his chest and slowly reach for his waistline. His body stiffens, and I hesitate.

He lifts himself to meet my eyes. "I guess you wouldn't know if you've ever done this before," his voice is husky and uncertain, hovering above me.

"It doesn't matter." I shake my head, breathing hard.

His eyes fill with doubt.

"I want this. I want you, Ryder," I say a little too desperately.

After a few moments, he leans down and plants a gentle kiss on my lips before reluctantly lifting himself up and lying beside me. I can feel my heart breaking as he moves away from me, until he pulls me close and kisses my forehead.

"We have to wait," he says softly.

My heart beats painfully, heating my cheeks with colors of rejection. "Why?"

"Because I don't have protection and I want you to be sober before we do anything you might regret."

"I would never regret being with you." I look up at him in protest, my stomach suddenly turning with nausea.

He combs his fingers through my hair. "Still, I want our time together to be perfect," he says into my ear below a whisper.

I go limp against him, stubbornly accepting defeat. I breathe deeply and nuzzle my face into his chest, closing my eyes and ignoring the spinning behind the dark of my eyelids.

CHAPTER 25

12 years ago Ryder

I'm so lonely, so very very lonely.

I sing along to the song that plays on repeat in the large room. The folk melody gets quieter as it comes to an end and then louder as it starts back up again.

She was my girl... My dearest friend...and I'm no longer alone...

I know every single word, note, every single change in key and rhythm. It's a song of friendship, love, and loneliness. I used to hate it. It used to drive me mad that it was never ending, always playing, over and over again. That is until I finally drowned it out. I learned how to shut off my mind and become numb to it, pretending it wasn't there. But when that stopped working and I couldn't escape its constant sound anymore, I decided to actually listen to it and understand the words.

So very, very lonely.

Just as the song says, I think I am lonely. I've only ever known this place, but it is a lonely place. I don't know why they keep me here. I don't know why they keep this song on repeat while I lay strapped to this metal bed alone, but it's become a comfort to me, my only friend. I hope to meet the man who sings this song someday. Maybe he'd be kind to me...

I can't take it anymore, this place. I'd rather not exist than have to spend another second here. The scary man rarely comes to see me now. I'm only occasionally visited by the rubber suits who say nothing to me other than, "Pathetic *Rider,*" before they put needles into me or put me to sleep.

I don't want to be alone anymore... *I just wish I had someone to talk to.*

The music cuts off.

Relief and fear spread through me. The song never stops playing; when it does, it only means one thing. The scary man is coming.

As if on cue, the creaking metal door swings open. His long shadow casts along the tile floor long before his fingers wrap around the door and he peers inside. He always has the same look on his face. *A fake smile... Fake skin.* I don't know why those words always ring inside my head when I see him. At some point I convinced myself his face wasn't real… But I know that isn't true. *It was just a bad dream.*

Fear works its way inside me as he stations himself to his favorite place in the room— right by my side. What does he plan to do with me today? The thought makes me sick to my stomach. I can't stand any more of it… The pain, the loneliness. I don't want to be alone anymore.

I stare up at the ceiling as he works around my freshly cleaned body. An orange suit just recently scrubbed me down with a wet rag, that should have been a clear indication. I should have guessed he was coming.

I feel cold pokes and sharp pricks as he works his way up. Before they always felt much more painful, but now they're just more annoying than anything.

He stops to untie my restraints, an act which is very rarely done. I brace myself for the worst, knowing the familiar needle and IV all too well, but instead he lays my arms back to my sides, still free from restraints. I have to resist the urge to rub my wrists and stretch my arms. I am not allowed relief or comfort in this place.

This stupid place.

I think… I think I want to die.

A bubble forms in my throat. For the first time, that thought has brought me nothing but a feeling of peace. I've wanted to live and keep fighting for more in the past, but I know nothing more exists outside of this. I have to accept that. Everything from the song is a lie. There isn't love… There isn't friendship… There's nothing.

Without thinking, I search the small room with my eyes. There has to be some way... My eyes land on a small scalpel lying on the metal tray to my left.

I focus on the scalpel, careful not to drag the man's attention to my face.

Would it really be so bad... to be free from this place? Free of the fear and pain, free of it all...

The man turns away from me to grab something. *Now's my only chance.*

I grab the scalpel, my arm almost failing as I beg it to move. I bring it to my neck and press until I feel its sharp bite, followed by the warmth of blood. I hold it there. The man turns to face me again and his eyes widen.

For the first time, his face changes. *Now he's the one who looks scared.*

"What are you doing, *rider*?"

"I—" My voice catches in my throat. I never get to speak.

"Put that down," he growls.

I swallow, my arm feeling weaker as my confidence starts to dwindle.

Please... I can't give up now.

"You're making a big mistake. Are you really prepared to face the consequences?" He steps closer. My arm holding the scalpel is just out of his reach.

I tighten my grip, pressing the blade deeper into my neck. "Yes. I— I can't live like this anymore." I choke on my words, barely able to get them out.

He takes another step and goes to grab my arm.

"Don't!" I scream. The moment his fingers touch my skin, he freezes.

I look up at him, waiting for the inevitable to happen, but he doesn't move.

"Wh— what do you want?" He gasps out.

He can't move...

I don't understand. "What?"

"Tell me, what is it that you want? I will give it to you. Just please put the blade down." he says, his face strained.

"What do I want?" I repeat, confusion pulling on my brows.

"Yes, tell me. I will make it better for you here."

My grip around the blade loosens. Tears well up around my eyes. I've never been given a choice before. I've never gotten something that I wanted. There's only one thing I can think of, only one thing that I want.

"I don't want to be alone anymore."

***

For the first time, I wake up somewhere new. Instead of a flat metal surface, I'm lying on cold wet rock, and though it's not any more comfortable, I can actually *move*.

I stare at my hands and legs, free from any restraints. I stretch them out, cracking every joint, wiggling every toe and finger.

And it's quiet. No song playing, nothing. I don't realize I'm crying until drops splatter onto my hands. *Where am I?*

"Hey, are you okay?" A voice startles me.

I look up. Across from me are metal bars and a woman huddled against them.

I've never seen a woman before...

She has long black hair, brown skin, and strange writing on her arm.

CHAPTER 26

Maze

I wake up slowly, a slight throbbing pain ping-ponging between my temples. I scan the van with my eyes and groan loudly once I realize I'm alone. Embarrassment tugs at my insides as the memories from the night before swarm my mind.

I should have never thrown myself at him like that. It felt right in the moment with logic blurred by alcohol. But now I can't shake this feeling that I did something wrong. That I lost control. *I am never drinking again.*

The sick feeling swimming in my stomach solidifies the thought.

Regardless, I hope that whatever feelings or affection Ryder might have had for me last night are still there. Although I feel ashamed and embarrassed for how

I acted, I have to admit that my feelings were real. They *are* real. I had wanted to be with him last night, the night before, and every night before that. I just wish I had done it differently.

After a long emotional war between me and myself, I notice a water bottle sitting beside the bed with a piece of paper underneath it. My stomach flutters as I pick it up and read:

"Hope you're feeling okay this morning. Make sure to drink this water. Me and Richard went shopping for the day, be back soon.

Love, Ryder :)"

I sigh with relief. The note makes me feel more hopeful that I didn't make a complete fool of myself. I grab the water bottle and step out of the van at a sluggish pace. Hunger and nausea pull at my legs. I make my way toward the house, dragging my feet along the way and kicking up dust from the dry ground.

Once I'm inside, I try to fight the pounding headache as I navigate the kitchen. There's not much food left to choose from. I pop a couple pieces of bread into the toaster and pour myself a cup of coffee from the electric pot— still warm from when it was brewed this morning.

This is the first time they've ever left me here alone. Ryder usually goes on the shopping trips by himself, leaving Richard and me here to paint the day away. I must admit that part of me is glad they're both gone. I need some time to get my thoughts in order and figure out what I will say to Ryder when he gets back. *"Sorry that I was drunk and stupid last night and tried to jump your bones?"* I don't know...

I sit at the same table from the night before as I eat my toast. Besides the jars of weed, the table is cluttered with stacks of newspapers and old junk, coated in dust from sitting in place too long. It makes me wonder if Richard would ever let me help clean up and organize around here one day. Probably not. He made it clear that he hates change, and I'm sure that having the house cleaned for once would send him right over the edge.

My eyes study the gloomy house, hoarded with all its old junk and worn-out furniture. There's not a single framed family photo or knick-knack that would reveal an ounce of sentiment. It makes me feel somewhat sorry for Richard and that he chose such a life of solitude. It also makes me worry for him once we leave for Alaska. I hate having to leave him here alone again. I hope that Ryder will want us to return someday soon after.

My stomach twists with sadness and nausea.

The thought of leaving this place behind makes me feel more than a little depressed. It may not be much, but at some point, I realized that the small life we built here does mean something to me. All of the quiet early mornings with coffee before work in the greenhouse, music playing while Ryder and I dance around and work for hours. And then when evening comes, all of us will meet for dinner around the fire and talk about our day.

I've grown to love our simple, familiar day-to-day life.

I finish my toast and coffee and take the dishes to the sink. Once I finish washing them, I stand in place for a few moments, unsure what to do with myself. I walk back over to the table and stare at the dozens of jars. A small hint of pride bounces into my chest. I really hope that whoever gets the pleasure of buying and smoking this weed can somehow feel the time and effort Ryder and I put into it. *Together.*

As I admire each jar, I spot a glass pipe sitting beside them, the same one Richard will smoke from throughout the day. Curiosity itches at my fingertips as I pick it up. There's unburnt weed inside the bowl that Richard is either saving for later or has forgotten about. Most likely saving for later...

The small throbbing pain in my head continues. I know I shouldn't, but it makes me wonder if smoking it would somehow help, as I recount all the times Richard would instantly relax whenever he smoked from it. And from what little knowledge I have, I know that weed is often used to relieve pain.

I hold the glass pipe for a while as I nervously glance at the windows to ensure they're not back yet. The longer I take to decide, the sooner they'll be here. Finally, I go for it.

How bad could it be?

I grab the lighter from the kitchen counter and hold it up to the pipe, mimicking all the times I've seen Richard do it before. I light it and inhale. The hot smoke fills my lungs and I try to hold it in for a moment but they quickly give out, releasing the smoke and leaving me in a fit of coughs.

Maybe this wasn't such a good idea...

My hands shake slightly as I set the pipe down where I found it and take a small piece of bud from one of the jars, putting it into the pipe bowl to replace what I had smoked. I figure whatever Richard doesn't know won't hurt him. *I hope.*

I sit for a few minutes waiting to feel out the effects. Once I decide it's probably safe to assume that nothing is going to happen, I stand up. Instantly my body sways and the room seems to shift all around me. I quickly sit back down, my body feeling heavy as it sinks into the chair. I try to relax my increasing heart rate and steady my breath, but every touch and movement I make vibrate and linger against my skin. My heart rate picks up as I lay my head against the table and wait for the panic to subside.

After a few moments drag on, my nerves suddenly calm and my panicked heart rate is put to rest. I slowly stand back up as my mind acclimates to the swaying sensation. *I definitely won't be doing that again.*

My mouth goes dry. I try to look around for where I left the water bottle but my body moves slowly and the swaying makes it hard to get around. Once I finally find it on the counter, I chug the rest— a euphoric wave washing over me. *That's probably some of the best water I have ever had...* My headache also seems to have disappeared like I hoped, and the floating sensation doesn't feel as scary as it did before.

Before my brain has time to catch up, my feet amble toward the garage on their own. I figure that I might as well paint to try and distract myself and pass the time.

I set up a new canvas on the stand and sit in front of it. Completely paralyzed to the seat, my body instantly refusing to move. My brain feels like pudding and I can't seem to find the motivation to move my hands toward the paint. My eyes glaze over as I glance at the wall and the many paintings leaning up against it. It really is amazing how many Richard and I have done in the last few weeks I've been here. He has a more abstract and colorful style compared to mine. For some reason I like using different variations of black and recreating the sky.

Maybe I'll try something different today.

I look back at the canvas and it doesn't take much time before I finally grab the paintbrush and start painting away. The familiar feeling of being entranced takes over me, but this time it somehow feels even more enhanced and magical than before. I can see why Richard enjoys this so much, smoking and painting, as inspiration spews through me like a carefully choreographed yet chaotic dance.

Time seems to drag on and yet speed up as my hands make their way from wet paint to canvas and back in beautiful tradition. Hours pass once I finally finish. Sore from sitting in place too long, I stretch my arms out and crack my neck.

Standing up, I step back to take in my finished work. It's different from all the others I've done before, yet it means so much more to me. It's of Ryder, and somehow,

I captured his brilliant smile and his warm, but piercing brown eyes. I started painting him before I realized what I was doing; by then, it was too late. I sigh deeply as I stare at it. I just hope he doesn't mind.

The effects from the weed have already worn off, allowing me to think clearly and bringing back all my worries about the night before. I just hope that if anything, we can just pretend it never happened and go back to normal.

But truly, I don't think I want it to go back to normal...

I leave the garage and begin walking toward the house. There I notice Richard's truck is back and parked in the driveway. A bolt of anxious surprise shoots through me. *How long have they been back?* I must have been really sucked into my painting to not even hear them pull up.

I walk up to the front door, preparing myself to act as normal as possible. It's time to face Ryder and talk about what happened last night, and also face Richard and just hope for the life of me that he doesn't find out what I did. I reach to open the door but pause when I hear the loud roaring of Richard's voice.

I stand frozen in place. How did he discover that I smoked his weed already? *God, he's gonna kill me...*

"That's why you wanted to go shopping every time, isn't it!?" he yells, and for the first time since I met him, he sounds truly angry.

Ryder's voice muffles in and out. "Can you please just keep your voice down?"

Okay, maybe this isn't about the weed...

"Don't fucking tell me what to do! This is serious, really fucking serious, Ryder. When were you gonna tell her? Never? Hell— when were you gonna tell me?"

I have never heard Ryder or Richard sound like this before. The volume and tone of their voices sends chills through me.

"I was trying to figure it out, okay? You don't understand, Richard. She's like me. I was trying to make her remember." Ryder's voice sounds panicked and desperate.

Whatever this is about, it's really bad...

"There you go again with that bullshit. I don't care where you say you're from or whatever delusions you believe in. Her face was plastered on the missing persons wall! We could both go to jail for this! Don't you understand? You need to call the police!"

"Please just give me some more time. She doesn't belong with those people."

"You mean with her family! Fucking Christ, Ryder. Are you the one who kidnapped her?"

What—

"No! Please, Richard. You have to trust me. I've always done right by you. Just let me leave with her tonight and we'll never come back. It'll be like we were never here. I promise you."

They both grow quiet as I step away from the door, unable to stomach hearing anymore of it.

The Forgetful Rain

The world around me is spinning. I back away from the house, each of my limbs almost failing to hold me up. Before I'm able to collapse, I turn to run.

CHAPTER 27

Ryder

I slide the keys into the ignition and turn. The van sputters to life and the purr of her engine is like being welcomed by an old friend. *The sweet sound of freedom.*

The van is exactly how I left it. All the furniture is still in place, my cash is still in the glovebox, and the tiny dream catcher is still hanging from the rearview mirror. It looks the same as it did when I had last seen it, frozen in time. Except for a fine layer of dust that coats every surface, it's as if I never lost it.

I thought that it was destroyed or lost forever after they recaptured me. I never thought I would ever see it again. I try to shake away the haunting memory of that shitty day, but it crashes into me with full force.

At first, it was a normal day. Dude and I were camping out on the southern border of Arizona. Taking a breather after a long trip. My plan was for us to get to Mexico and figure it out as we went. I wanted to get us away from the facility, as far south as the earth would allow. But obviously you can't get very far on wheels, and I knew it would be almost impossible to get us on a boat or plane.

We were alone, in the middle of nowhere— parked in some deserted unmarked campground. Dude was running back and forth, bringing me the biggest sticks he could find and wagging his tail ecstatically every time I approved of one and praised him. That was his favorite thing to do.

I still can't get over how smart he was...

I remember lounging back on the picnic table while reading a book I had picked up somewhere in Utah. The book was a bizarre mystery and I was really sucked into it. Dude had given up his stick-finding mission and padded over to me, nudging me with his wet nose to get my attention.

At first, I didn't know why, but then I felt it. Something was wrong. I knew Dude could feel it too because his ears were suddenly pinned back against his head and he cowered behind me with his tail between his legs. Dude always knew when something was wrong. I should have been paying closer attention...

Then, without a second more to react. We were suddenly swarmed by their soundless aircrafts. They materialized in the sky, as if they had been there all along but were camouflaged. The aircrafts were large and terrifying. Faster than a blink of the eye, they landed just as silently as they appeared. A force of nature that no one could ever detect.

It was like watching a horrific car accident, or something worse. Something that sticks with you forever.

I tried to run as fast as possible to get to the van and get me and Dude out of there, but I couldn't get very far. They appeared out of thin air and surrounded me. There was nowhere for me to go. I tried to yell for Dude to run and get away but he wouldn't listen as they grabbed hold of my arms. They zapped me with their weapons, making me fall to my knees as they restrained my arms behind my back. I tried to fight them off but there was nothing I could do. There were too many of them and they came prepared.

I watched as Dude ran after me, biting at one of the men's legs dragging me away before the man finally got tired of it and grabbed him by his neck and threw him away from us. Dude landed on his side. I could hear his whimper in the distance but thankfully he wasn't hurt, that much I could tell. If he were, I don't know what I would have done... I would never forgive myself. But the look on his face was painful enough to watch, as he tried to keep up and they continued to drag me farther away. He tried to follow even when I was put into the aircraft and even after I was lifted into the sky, he never gave up.

I could see him below as the aircraft hovered above. He circled the ground where I had just been, looking up in search of me in the sky. Waiting for my return.

I never got a chance to say goodbye...

And I'll never know what happened to him. If he was found by someone else and taken in to be their new best friend, or if he continued to wander the desert looking for me until he couldn't wander anymore...

The painful memory brings a lump to my throat. I don't understand how they found me. Why right then? Why not sooner? I had escaped for over a year and there was never any sign of them before then. How the hell did they do it?

I breathe slowly, forcing the lump down and pushing the memory to the side. None of that matters now. Now I'm free. Now I finally get to leave after all these years, without worrying about them capturing me again. True freedom at last.

Now I have to find her.

I can feel her. Lingering inside me, just the faintest hint of something foreign, yet feels as though it somehow belongs. I can feel it tugging on me, pulling me toward her like an invisible thread connected between us. More images of desert flash through my mind. She's walking now which makes it harder to follow. *Where is she going?*

I drive the van in the direction I'm being pulled to. It's definitely getting harder now that she's moving. Luckily though, it seems driving comes just as naturally to me despite how long it's been. It comes just as easily as the day I had first done it. *The day Richard had taught me how.*

The sun that's shining through the windshield warms my skin. I squint to see past it, my eyes burn with sensitivity to it, but it doesn't bother me. It's been too long since I've seen or felt natural sunlight. It's been too long since I breathed clean air or felt a breeze brush against my skin. Any amount of pain is worth this freedom.

Nothing could compare to this. *Absolutely nothing-*

Her face interrupts my thoughts and intrudes my mind. Her smile... her voice...

My heart beats painfully.

I'm getting closer now. The connection feels stronger. It's almost as if I can hear her thoughts and feel her feelings.

She's distressed, weak, and— Something isn't right.

She doesn't feel like herself... If that makes sense? No, something is definitely off.

The closer I get to her the more her presence intensifies, pulling me in with a force I just can't shake.

I pull into a gas station parking lot to calm myself and get my thoughts in order. I also figure if she's as hungry as I am right now (and I'm fucking starving), she'll at least be thankful I brought something to eat and drink... It's the least I can do.

I glance down at what I'm wearing. I don't know how long I've been wearing the same T-shirt and jean shorts. They're covered in dirt and muck and I know for a fact, I don't smell pretty. I hop into the back of the van, grab a clean olive-green shirt and jean shorts, and change into them quickly. I have to move fast. She's been walking for a while now and I don't know how much further she'll go.

After changing, I scramble to stuff my pocket with cash from the glovebox before getting out of the van and attempting to walk normally— meaning not like someone who has been locked up in an underground facility for God knows how long— into the gas station.

I open the door and take everything in. It may just be a normal gas station to some, with plenty of snacks, candy, and beer stocking the many shelves. But to me it's a breath of fresh air compared to where I have been trapped for most of my life.

The cashier behind the counter lifts his head from his phone, eyes me up and down before returning his attention to the screen in his hands. I breathe out a sigh of relief that I don't look abnormal to him or look like a cause for suspicion. *And man is it nice to see a new face for once...*

My mouth waters as I grab plastic-wrapped sandwiches from a see-through fridge and cold bottled waters. Before I can get a chance to stop myself, I rip open the packaging of one of the sandwiches and stuff my face with it as I stand in the aisle. I scarf it down quickly as though it might disappear right out of my hands.

Once I finish, I open and chug an entire bottle of water. *God, I missed this.* As I chug the water, my eyes close involuntarily with satisfaction, completely engulfed in my own pleasurable world. I don't notice the gas station clerk is gawking at me until he clears his throat to get my attention.

I lower the water bottle from my mouth.

"You know you have to pay for those right?" He says, obviously annoyed with his life.

"Oh yeah, no problem. I was just real hungry. You know how it is." I shrug, trying to act as normal as possible. I follow him back to the check-out counter and watch as he rings me up. "So uh, anything cool happenin in the world lately?"

The scrawny cashier peers up at me, lifting a single eyebrow. "Not really..."

I scratch my head and look away, trying to dissolve some of the awkwardness polluting the small gas station. I hadn't realized how rusty my normal conversation skills were.

Finally, he finishes bagging up the water and sandwiches and gives me a long look without saying anything.

"Cool, thanks!" I call behind me, taking the bag and rushing out the store.

She's moving quicker now. Images of a large windshield enter my mind. It looks like she is no longer walking and is now in some vehicle.

I hurry in a panic to start the van back up and get moving toward her as quickly as possible. I race down the narrow desert highway, I know it well and recognize the area almost immediately. I slow down when I feel her abruptly come to a stop and can feel myself drawing closer.

No longer than five minutes later, I pull into a lone parking lot in the middle of the desert. There sits a small building with a large old sign that has chipped paint with the word "Cafe" displayed. I park on the side of the building to stay out of sight and give myself some time to settle my racing thoughts.

This is it.

My body is trembling. What do I say to her when I see her? How do I explain to her how I got away and convince her to come back with me? *She'll never buy it...*

Do I really want to go through with this? Can I?

Either way I have to see her. The pulling need is almost physically painful and I don't think I could turn around and leave now. Even if I wanted to.

I flip down the mirror in front of me and get a good look at myself for the first time in what feels like years. My face is dirty and my hair is longer than I remember it being.

I grab a water bottle from the back and wet my hands before scrubbing the dirt off of my cheeks and combing my fingers through my hair.

Not too shabby...

After a few moments, I calm some of the trembling within my nerves. I draw in a deep breath before I finally step out of the van.

I try to walk steadily to the front door, placing one shaky foot in front of the other. I have to be brave. There's no turning back now. Somehow right now, the fear coursing through me at the thought of having to face her again is even more terrifying than Cock-eye or any of his orange minions could ever be. What if she sees right through me? What if this connection goes both ways and she's able to unravel me at my seams and reveal the facade?

I'm only a few feet away when I suddenly feel her distress increase drastically.

Panicking, I quickly open the front door and rush inside.

And there she is. Her back is turned toward me, but I know it's her. She looks so different against a setting that isn't concrete walls and based around fear. Her body is frail and she's covered in dirt, but she's beautiful. The most beautiful thing I have ever seen.

There are no metal bars separating us, no orange guards surrounding us and keeping us away from each other. For the first time, nothing keeping us apart.

CHAPTER 28

Maze

I run toward the van, my feet almost failing me more than once. Tears sting the corner of my eyes as I reach the van door. I fall to my knees, the weight of my small world collapsing on top of me. *Kidnapped? Family? Jail? How could this be happening?*

I try to wrap my head around it. I try with every inch of my being to make sense of it all. Standing up shakily, my head spins with nausea and the taste of bile reaches the back of my throat. I get into the passenger seat, my body trembling as I shut the door and lock it.

What am I supposed to do? I take short gasps of air into my lungs, trying desperately to calm myself. There has to be some sort of mistake, some sort of explanation for what I heard. Ryder would never hide something like this from me. He would never do anything to hurt me. I refuse to believe it.

Would he?

I manage to stop my hands from shaking and after a few moments, I force myself to finally think clearly. Whatever I heard, I need to find out for myself. I need to know the truth.

I rummage through the middle compartment between the front seats and find nothing but receipts, napkins and other pieces of garbage. I then open the compartment in front of me and there sits a phone.

His phone.

I hold my breath as I grab it and press the side button to turn it on. The bright screen flashes, revealing a picture of Ryder and a golden furred dog with chocolate brown eyes, by his side. *Dude.* They're both smiling big and Dude has his tongue hanging out of his mouth, looking just as goofy as I imagined him to be.

The picture causes the lump in my throat to thicken but I try to swallow it down. This is no time for reminiscing. At this point anything could be a lie. I want to trust Ryder, I really do. But if what I heard is true... Then anything that Ryder has told me since I met him could be a lie. I don't know what I will do if that is the case.

I swipe open the phone, relieved that there's no passcode. My fingers seem to navigate the phone better than I would have thought. They move around the screen with perfect muscle memory.

My thumb presses the safari app and goes to tap the search-bar at the top, but quickly freezes when I see the article's title already opened.

"The search continues for 2 missing girls outside of Las Vegas."

Time freezes. Everything around me disappears but the screen and myself. I can't get my eyes to look away.

My breathing hitches when I scroll down and see a picture of my face and another of a girl I don't recognize. I don't realize I'm crying until I feel tears stream down my face while I read.

*"Families of teens, **Maze Fontana**,19, and **Stacey Johnson**,19, plead with the community asking anyone who has any information that could lead to the girls' location to please come forward. The teen girls went missing in early September of last year after Johnson's car was found abandoned on the side of the road 4 hours outside of Las Vegas. It is believed that the girls got lost and stranded in the Mojave Desert, or were picked up by someone unknown. If anyone has any information, please call the number below."*

At the bottom of the article are pictures of what I presume are our families. In the first picture with the description that reads, "Mother and sister of Maze Fontana," stands a thin woman with numb eyes, her mouth pressed into a hard line. Next to her is a young girl frowning, with tears staining her small cheeks. I don't recognize either of them, but I can see the uncanny resemblance.

I try to fight back more tears as I scroll down.

In the next picture, the other girl's parents hold each other, staring at the ground with agonized faces.

My heart aches unbearably as I stare at the pictures. Nothing could have prepared me for this truth. This whole time I was convinced that somehow, I didn't have any family, that whoever I had known before losing my memory, had to have been bad people that hurt me and left me in the desert to die.

My hand instinctively reaches around and rubs my lower back where the large bruise used to be, but is now mostly healed.

Now that I think about it, I only thought those things because of Ryder. He's the one that put it in my head that I had no one else to turn to. He's the one that fed me all of those lies. All this time, he kept the truth from me and fed me bullshit.

Without thinking, my bottom lip quivers as I take a deep breath and dial the number from the bottom of the article. I press the phone to my ear.

It rings twice before a woman's voice answers. "Missing persons unit, how may I help you?"

I take another deep inhale through my nose, urging myself to speak.

"Hello? Missing persons unit, can you hear me?" she says again.

"Yes, hello," I finally say.

"Hello, how can I help you?" She repeats.

"My name is Maze Fontana. I am a missing person," I manage to say as I read the name labeled under the picture of my face. The line goes quiet for a moment.

"Ms. Fontana, can you tell me where you are? Are you safe?" she says, her voice more urgent.

"I don't know where I am. I think I'm safe. I don't know what to do." I sob out, everything starting to hit me all at once.

"Okay, listen to me, Maze. Try to stay calm, okay? We're going to find you."

Suddenly, the driver's side door swings open. I quickly hang up.

"Rainy?" Ryder says, panting. He looks at me then the phone in my hand. "Are you okay? Who were you talking to?"

My blood boils as I stare at him, anger and betrayal gripping at my lungs. I say nothing.

I trusted you.

I put the phone into my pocket as he slides into the driver's seat, shutting the door beside him. "Listen, I don't know what you heard or saw but you have to let me explain," he says slowly, his voice desperate.

Still, I say nothing. My mind is too clouded, and pain is stitching my mouth shut.

He says nothing else and starts the engine. The van begins to roll backwards. Every part of me starts to panic.

"Where are we going?" I ask quickly, searching the farm desperately with my eyes for any sign of Richard. I reach for the door but Ryder stops me. He presses the brake, making the van come to a stop.

"Please, Rainy. You have to trust me. I know you don't remember anything, but you have to believe me. I would never do anything to hurt you."

"Don't fucking call me that!" I snap back, anger spewing from my lips. "How could I ever trust you? You lied to me about everything! This whole time I thought you cared about me... It was all a lie." My voice breaks into sobs but I try to force them away.

He shakes his head, his eyes pleading. "I do care about you!"

I interrupt before he can continue. "And Alaska? This whole time you made me believe we were going there for an adventure but really you were just trying to get me far away so I'd never find out who I really was, weren't you? That's why you didn't tell Richard about it, isn't it? So, he wouldn't know where we were!" I yell out as everything starts to make sense.

He looks at me, tears forming around his eyes. "Please just let me explain everything. I can prove to you that I'm not lying. Just let me drive us out of here and I will show you the truth."

The look in his eye's tugs at something in my heart, causing some of the anger to dissolve. I grip the phone in my pocket, its presence bringing me a small sense of security.

"Fine." I breathe out, my voice still coated with distrust. "I will give you this one chance to prove to me why I should trust anything you say. But if you try to pull anything, I swear to god I will make sure you are arrested and held responsible."

He lets out a breath of relief. "Thank you," he says as he lifts his foot from the brake pedal and pulls the van away from the farm. As I watch the farm disappear, something inside me breaks and is replaced with numbness. I know it's the last time I will ever see it.

We drive for some time in silence. The sun begins to descend past the horizon, casting hues of orange light across our faces.

I don't know if I've made a terrible mistake by agreeing to go with him. He doesn't seem violent or malicious, actually everything he's ever done has always felt genuine. That's what makes this so hard to grasp. I don't know what to believe anymore...

No. I can't allow him to fool me again. I'll let him explain himself only so I can understand why he did this. For closure, but that's it.

"Well, are you gonna start explaining?" I finally say.

He inhales deeply as if what he's about to say is too painful. "Okay, now I know this might be hard to understand or even believe, but you have to bear with me. Okay?"

I nod my head once, eyeing him carefully as he begins.

"When we first met at that cafe, it wasn't actually the first time. We met over a year ago in the same— Um, facility."

"Facility?"

"Yes. It was like an imprisonment for people like us."

"People like us?" My voice repeats back in a distrusting tone, urging him to elaborate.

He pauses and studies me for a long moment then continues. "I didn't know how you got there because when you did, your memory was wiped then, too. They tend to do that whenever they get ahold of new *specimens.*

"We were both locked up in cells across from each other and got to know each other as time passed. Then after the experiments started on you, we learned the truth. After that, we came up with an escape plan. But when we finally succeeded, we were separated and somehow they wiped your memory again."

"So then, how did you end up there?" I interrupt, playing along with his bullshit story.

"Somehow, I escaped two years ago when Richard found me. I don't have much memory from before then, but after I stayed with him and healed him, I took off. They eventually found me again."

His words spread goosebumps across my skin as I remember when he told me that Richard once had cancer that miraculously went away after they met. More questions bounce around in my head. I don't want to believe him, I know that I shouldn't, but the tone in his voice makes it hard not to get pulled in.

"So, you escaped twice?"

He nods.

"And how exactly did you heal him? What truth did we find out?" I ask slowly.

He takes a deep, hesitant breath.

"Tell me," I demand.

"We found out that we're not from here... This planet, I mean," he says in a low, uncertain voice.

My body goes numb, rejecting every notion.

I knew this was a bad idea. Why the hell did I agree to go with him? Why do I continue to not listen to my instincts?

I shake my head. "You're insane."

"Rainy, please. You have to remember! We have to get out of here before they find us again!"

Hot tears cascade over my cheeks, I'm unable to stop them now. Why was I stupid enough to trust him in the first place? My heart rate picks up as all the memories and everything that led from the moment I met him until now, and all the choices I made in that time, flash through my mind. It was all a mistake.

I wish I never met him...

"Pull over!" I scream with force.

CHAPTER 29

Maze

To my surprise, Ryder immediately screeches the van to a stop.

I get out and slam the van door behind me, storming away. My body trembles with fear and anger as I walk away from the road and into the only truth I've ever known, the desert.

"Rainy, please get back in the van!" Ryder's voice calls after me. I ignore him and continue walking, my heartbeat drumming so loud in my ears that I almost don't hear him follow behind me. He grabs my wrist. "I know it's hard for you to believe, but if you just let me take you back there, I know it will trigger something in you and make you remember."

"I'm not going anywhere with you!" I snatch my wrist back from him. "You really expect me to believe that we're what? Aliens?!"

Maybe he really is crazy. The look in his eyes says he truly believes his own lies, but I know better now. All this time, I trusted him. I have to admit that I even had the smallest hope that he could somehow prove to me that he did all of this for a reason. I hoped that he lied for a reason, and that all this was just some big misunderstanding. I thought maybe we could go back to the farm and return to normal. That's partly why I agreed to go with him, to hear him out. For the smallest bit of hope that it would all work out in the end...

I was wrong.

I really started to fall for him... I *did* fall for him. But now I know that whoever Ryder is, he's not the person I met at that cafe and began to fall in love with. That person doesn't exist.

"Please, just listen to me. I'm just trying to protect you. I know you don't remember, but I promised to always protect you and stay by your side. Every day that we've finally been free together has been hell trying to make you remember again." He tries to step closer to me.

"I don't want to hear any more of your lies!" I scream, covering my ears with both hands and stepping back. I squeeze my eyes shut, wishing myself far away from this place, and that everything made sense. Even wishing away my own existence so that the strangers from those photos wouldn't be hurt by my disappearance. And most of all, wishing that Ryder was the person I thought he was.

A deep pressure pulses against my skull, making it hard to think.

When I open my eyes again, Ryder stands very still. His eyes heavy with pain and desperation. It makes me sick to my stomach knowing that those same eyes looked at me only a day before with something you could almost call love. And to think I really fell for it, I really thought he was someone I could find a future with. Once again, the painful truth is, I was wrong.

I look away. The sight of him filling hatred into my every limb.

"I didn't know you were missing," he whispers.

I scoff. All of his attempts to persuade me are now starting to really piss me off. "I saw the article on your phone," I spit.

"I know— I mean that, I didn't know until we got to the farm. I wanted to tell you; believe me I really did. I just wanted you to remember first. I didn't want to lose you..."

I stare at him silently, my mouth tasting of disgust, the pain morphing into numbness.

"Just think about it for a second, please. You woke up in the desert almost a month ago but you went missing over a year ago. Where do you think all of that time went? I promise you, I'm telling the truth," He pleads.

I narrow my eyes at him, my mind too clouded with betrayal to listen to a single word he says. He opens his mouth to say more but instead, the sudden sound of sirens goes off in the distance.

We both freeze as they quickly inch closer. He looks at me, his face full of panic. "You called the police?"

I shake my head, remembering the phone call I made earlier. I pull the phone out from my pocket as the realization hits me. We both stare at it in my hand.

"They tracked us," Ryder grits through his teeth.

Within moments, bright flashing lights and police cars surround us in the darkness.

I fall to my hands and knees as I'm overcome with different emotions, and for whatever reason, a small sense of guilt.

The pressure inside my head intensifies as everything crumbles inside of me with loss. The truth solidifies that the short life I've built for myself has now come to an end. Pain and grief crash into me as I slowly begin to understand the weight of losing everything I've ever known and cared for. All the memories I've created and cherished of the farm, of Richard... *And Ryder.* Now diminished to nothing.

I'd give anything to go back.

The pressure suddenly stops.

A pair of hands gently wrap around my shoulders, pulling me out of my daze. I look up, my vision blurred by tears. I expect to see Ryder staring back at me, but instead, it's a policewoman with a kind face. She whispers incoherent words to calm me as she leads me to an ambulance.

My head spins while the chaos swallows me whole. EMT's swarm around me, checking my vitals while writing things down and asking different questions. I don't respond to them. My mind and body are too exhausted to comprehend or react to anything.

Soon, once the chaos begins to simmer down around me, two men appear in front of me wearing clean suits with ties and holding out their badges for me to see. "Ms. Fontana, we understand that this is a difficult time for you but we were hoping that you could answer a couple of our questions," the taller man says, his voice as rough as sandpaper.

My eyes stare past them, searching the area for Ryder amongst the crowd of people. I can't see him anywhere.

"Ms. Fontana, do you have any idea where Stacey Johnson might be?" The tall man asks, waiting for me to speak.

I divert my gaze back to them, my heart sinking low as I remember her name and the picture of her from the article. I shake my head.

The tall man writes something down then continues. "It's our understanding that the two of you were close and you were the last to see her, is that correct?"

I shake my head again. "I don't know. I don't remember."

Disappointment spreads across their faces as they stare at me. It's clear that they were expecting a different answer, one that I am unable to give.

"What's going to happen to Ryder?" I ask.

The men glance at each other then back to me. "To who?"

"The guy who was here with me."

"There was a man here with you?" The tall man repeats back.

"Yes, he was standing right next to me when you guys pulled up."

"We did not see anyone else here," the man states, concern pulling at his brows.

I sigh. "He must have taken off in his van then." The anger of his betrayal returns as I realize that after everything he's done, he has now abandoned me as well. *Fucking coward.*

The man pulls out a walkie-talkie from his belt and proceeds to speak into it. "Search the grounds for another individual. A man, goes by the name of Ryder. Also, I want a thorough search of the van and have it taken into custody."

My eyes widen. "The van is still here?"

"Yes, do not worry. We will make sure he is found and taken in for questioning."

I inhale sharply, a small hint of guilt tugging at my heart once again. I try to push it away. I try to remind myself that he doesn't deserve my guilt or any of the pain I've felt for that matter. The reminder sinks my insides with heavy numbness and dread. *Just last night, he meant everything to me...* Everything has changed so quickly.

A small woman walks up holding a clear plastic bag with what I can see has Ryder's phone inside of it. The men inspect it, then hold it up for me to see with the screen turned on showing the picture of Ryder and Dude. "Is this him?"

I hesitate, then nod my head yes. The man pulls out his walkie-talkie again and speaks into it. He gives a detailed description of what Ryder looks like and explains that he is now a person of interest. They then walk away, leaving me alone in the back of the ambulance with an EMT stationed by my side.

I sit silently, everything playing out in front of me like a horrific crime scene. Investigators carefully scour the grounds as if a single piece of dirt might solve the entire mystery. Policemen stand to the side, making phone calls while some seem to even congratulate each other and shake hands. As if right now would be a time for celebration, despite the fact that Stacey Johnson is still missing and I have zero memory of what happened to us.

I swallow hard, holding back more tears as I think about all the challenges I'm going to have to face, when everyone wants answers from me and I won't be able to give any to them. I try to think hard, begging my mind to reveal all my lost memories. But like all the attempts before, I'm given nothing more than a dizzy headache.

The men return. Their faces are somehow more serious than before. "Ms. Fontana, would you please come back with us to the station?" They ask me this as though I have a choice.

I reluctantly stand up and follow them to one of the police vehicles where they have me get into the back. "Were you able to find him?" I ask once the men get into the front seats and start driving away from the scene. I watch out the window as the crowd of people and emergency vehicles grow smaller and smaller, before disappearing amongst the darkness. Ryder's van was no longer where we had left it.

"No," one of them answers but it's too dark to see which. They leave it at that and something tells me they would be unwilling to say more.

I lean back against the seat; my mind and body numb and exhausted. It takes everything in me to try and force my eyes to stay open the longer we drive through the dark desert. Without realizing, I eventually lose the battle.

***

I'm running for my life... They're chasing us. If they catch us, we will die. I stare at the hand holding mine and glance up to see who it belongs to. The blurriness is starting to fade... Ryder.

I jolt awake once my body feels the car stop. I try to adjust my eyes to the surroundings but my eyelids are heavy and swollen from crying and lack of sleep.

The men open the car door for me and when I step out, I can see that we're in a large parking lot beside an even larger building. The sky is now painted with lighter shades of blue, suggesting an early morning.

We slowly walk toward the large gray building with dark windows.

"Let's take her in through the side to avoid the media," the shorter man tells the other. The other nods in agreement.

Shouts and commotion come from a crowd on the other side of the building. The men open up an inconspicuous door on the side and usher me inside.

The inside is spotless and warm. The air smells oddly of paper with hints of coffee. I follow them through a narrow hallway, our footsteps echoing as we walk.

They lead me to a large room. When I step through the threshold, it takes me a moment to register what I'm seeing. On a row of seats sits a group of people I quickly recognize from the photographs.

CHAPTER 30

Maze

A small girl runs into my arms and sobs into my chest. "Mazie, I thought I'd never see you again!" She manages to say between sobs. The frail woman from the photograph stands back, wide-eyed as she stares at me with all color drained from her face. After a few moments, the small girl pulls away. She looks up at me with tears and snot smeared across her face.

"I've missed you so much! Mom said you were never coming back. She said you were dead and never coming back." She shakes her head, her voice trembling.

"That's enough, Zaya." The woman scolds her quietly, her voice thick with an accent.

Zaya steps back, wiping her face with her shirt. "I'm sorry," she says.

The woman moves closer to me, inspecting me carefully as if I might disappear again if she makes any sudden movements. She then pulls me in for a hug. Her body is stiff and her arms feel unwelcoming around me, until she quickly drops them back down and steps away.

I watch them silently, failing to find the words that might bring them an ounce of peace or reassurance. I stand awkwardly, feeling like an imposter within my own skin as I watch these strangers mourn the lost time they've spent away from me, believing I was dead, when really, I have no idea what's happened to me or if I'll ever be the person they remember again. That person might as well be dead.

The couple I recognize from the other picture stand further back. They watch us as they cry quietly to themselves and wait patiently. The man comforts his wife, whispering softly to her and wiping away her tears. They both look as though they just got out of bed. They're still wearing pajamas and their hair is a tousled mess. The woman is beautiful, her skin is dark and her face is similar to her daughters from what I can remember from the photograph. Her husband is tall, with messy brown hair and pale white skin in contrast to the dark circles that hang under his eyes beneath his glasses.

They timidly make their way from across the room, their eyes desperate for answers.

"Maze, we are so happy to see you again. So happy you are home safely." The woman pauses, glancing at her husband and back at me before she continues. "We never thought we would see you again. We thought— We were both so worried about you and Stacey. Could you please tell us what happened? Do you know where Stacey is or how we can find her?" Her voice is raspy, full of hope.

I grip my arm, the familiar stinging in my eyes returning. How can I tell them the truth without shattering their entire existence? It's obvious by the looks of it that these people have once given up hope on ever seeing their daughter again, that this moment is a miracle come true for them. *Why do I have to be the one to break their hearts all over again?*

I shake my head, feeling more worthless than I ever have before. "I'm so sorry. I don't remember."

There's a moment of silence.

"What do you mean you don't remember?" The man blurts out, his voice harsh and full of disbelief.

His wife puts a gentle hand on top of his shoulder to calm him. "We understand that this is a really hard time for you. We just want to know that she's safe," she says softly with an apologetic look in her eyes.

Don't feel sorry for me. I'm useless.

Before I can say more, one of the men from the entrance of the room clears his throat. "We're sorry to have to interrupt, but Ms. Fontana needs to come back with us for more questioning."

"Right now?" Zaya argues. "But she just got back!"

"Yes, is that really necessary? She's obviously had a long night. She should be able to spend this time with her family before police bombard her." Stacey's mom chimes in.

"I'm sorry, but it is important we get all of the information we need regarding the case. Currently Ms. Fontana is under our custody until we have further evidence to show she is no longer a suspect."

"What the hell does that mean? Suspect of what?" Stacey's father interjects.

"That's all we can say for now." The men step forward, motioning me out of the room. I turn to follow them, not wanting to see the dreadful look on the unfamiliar faces any longer.

I feel a tug on my shirt before I can exit the room. I look over to see Zaya gripping my sleeve with more tears forming around her eyes. She wraps her arms around me, holding on tight. "Please don't leave again, Mazie. Please don't go."

For an instant, I'm not sure what to do with my arms or how to respond. I'm standing awkwardly, but then my hands instinctively reach up and caress her head.

I wish I could comfort this girl or be who she remembers me to be. It's clear that I'm very important to her and she was once important to me. I can feel it as I hold her.

"It's gonna be okay. I won't be long," I tell her softly, my heart beating painfully. The frail woman tugs her off of me, scolding her again. I turn away, too ashamed of myself to look at them. *I feel like a fraud.*

I follow the men outside of the room. Everything inside me is begging me to run, begging me to disappear.

I know I shouldn't, but a part of me wishes that I never called that missing persons number, that I was never found. Something tells me that it would have been easier on everyone if I had never come back. I can't be who they want me to be, and I can't help them find their daughter either. Me being here is only making things worse.

I follow the men into a small dark room, illuminated by one light. They tell me to sit down at the table. I do so and they ask if I need any food or water. I shake my head, my body too numb to want anything. They then sit down across from me, holding a stack of papers inside a folder.

The tall man opens one of the folders and rummages through several pages. "Okay Ms. Fontana, we're gonna start with some easy questions for you. Just try to answer them to the best of your ability, okay? First off, do you recognize this car?"

He holds up a picture of a silver jeep for me to see. I shake my head.

The seconds seem to drag on as he jots something down.

"This is Stacey Johnson's car. We have reason to believe that both you and Stacey were inside of it the night of your disappearance," he explains as he sets the picture down on the table so I can take a closer look at it.

I stare at the picture longer, hoping it might reveal something, anything at all. I breathe deeply, frustrated with myself. "I'm sorry, I still can't remember anything."

"What exactly do you remember of your disappearance?"

"All I can remember is waking up in the desert and finding my way to a cafe where I met Ryder."

"And how long ago was that?"

"Maybe a month ago."

The man rubs his head, eyeing me suspiciously. "So, you're saying, you don't recall anything at all before a month ago?"

"Yes; that's exactly what I'm saying. Nothing before my disappearance or after," I try to explain but they don't look convinced.

"Interesting..." The man trails off as he writes some more. He then looks back to me, his eyes darker and more vicious. "So, you and this man *Ryder* lived together in the van?"

"Yes." I don't mention anything about Richard or the farm. I don't want him to have to get wrapped up in this whole mess. I've ruined enough lives as it is.

"And did you know that the van was reported stolen over a year ago? Just before your disappearance."

My eyes widen. *What?*

"I did not. Ryder said it was his."

The room is quiet for a moment except for the sound of pen against paper.

"Well, given that we couldn't find a single trace of another person where we found you, we have reason to believe that Ryder does not exist," the man says coldly.

My breathing stops. "What? That's impossible."

"Is it possible that you could have accidentally done something to Stacey Johnson and conveniently convinced yourself to *forget* everything?"

I slam my hands on the table, standing up and letting the tears spill down my cheeks. "No! I would never do that!"

"How do you know? You said you forgot everything about who you are. How would you know what you're capable of?"

I sit back down slowly, the thought making me sick to my stomach. He's right, I don't know what I would and wouldn't do. I don't know anything. What if I did do something so unspeakable? The image of Stacey's parents crying and begging for answers comes to my mind, making me hyperventilate. I place my face into my hands, trying to keep it together as the room begins to spin around me.

Suddenly the door opens. I lift my face from my hands and watch as two more men step inside the small room.

"Excuse me? This is a private questioning. No one else is allowed inside this room," the tall man says sternly.

The two men standing at the door hold out their badges. They're wearing dark suits with unreadable expressions on their faces. They have dark eyes and their skin is oddly pale enough to look gray. "This case is under our jurisdiction now. We will be taking Maze Fontana with us and any other evidence you were able to obtain," one of them says as they step forward.

"What would give the federal government the right to this case?" The shorter man at the table speaks up.

"That's none of your concern." They respond coldly in unison as one grabs the paperwork off the table and the other grabs me by my arm, pulling me out of the seat.

I have a sick feeling in my stomach. *Who the hell are these guys?*

With a firm grip on my arm, they pull me outside the building and lead me toward a black SUV. I can still hear the loud yelling and commotion coming from a distance as they push me into the back of the car.

The inside smells clean with a hint of bleach and something else, something almost rotten and familiar. They silently get into the front seats and begin driving as I sit petrified, unsure of what to think or feel. I try to look out the window but the glass is tinted dark, completely black, preventing me from seeing out of it.

"Excuse me, could you please roll down the window? I don't feel so good," I say as the spinning in my head and stomach increases. They say nothing, sitting silently and stoned-faced toward the road.

Panic rises in my chest as I slowly begin to recognize the inside of the car and the familiar smell. I grip the seat;

my heart racing as random images begin to flood my mind.

A cold dark room…Metal bars…Glowing eyes…

"Could you please tell me where you're taking me?" I ask, my voice louder with panic. Still, they say nothing.

I turn toward the door and try to open it. My body shakes when it doesn't budge. I lay down, prepared to kick the window out with my foot when the man in the passenger seat turns around and grabs me by my hair. I try to scream but the man quickly covers my mouth and nose with a cloth. His face is still stone-cold, blank and expressionless. His eyes black and lifeless.

I gasp for air, struggling to breathe as I try to squirm away, but the man holds me firmly. My body goes limp as my vision begins to blur and images and memories continue to flood back. Everything goes black just as I realize that I remember.

I remember everything.

Epilogue

I hear his voice before I open my eyes. The rough nasally pitch of it sends a sharp fear through me, making me come to an immediate realization of where I am.

"How very fortunate for us to have found her before any more damage could be done. Now if we could only get ahold of that elusive *rider*, everything would be just perfect."

My body goes numb at the sound of his name. I think back to everything he told me right before I was taken… and how I didn't believe a single word of it. How I treated him like I hated him when all he was doing was trying to protect me.

The memories start to crash into me. All the moments inside of the cell, the love I started to feel, then the heartbreak when we were separated. I remember every second we spent apart before we were finally reunited again… The lake, the farm, Richard.

My mom… *Zaya.*

"Open your eyes, Nixie!"

I jolt to full consciousness, my heartbeat racing. Bright light blinds me from above as my eyes squint open.

"Ah, welcome home. You're finally right back where you belong." I can make out his dark eyes peering down at me before anything else, the blurriness slowly leaving my vision.

My body is strapped down and I'm unable to move. Surrounding Cock-eye are blurry figures. I first make out the orange-suited ones, but right beside him is someone new. But she's not new... I recognize her face. At first, everything about her looks the exact same, other than the neatly pressed suit fitted to her body and the blank expression on her face.

Then I notice her eyes. They're as dark and lifeless as the rest.

Oh. God. No. *Stacey.*

Ingram Content Group UK Ltd.
Milton Keynes UK
UKHW040945010623
422707UK00004B/102